LUCY'S LOOKING GLASS

Lucy's Looking Glass

LUKAS ALLEN

CONTENTS

| 1 |

The First Lesson: Lucy

Lucy

Lucy went to work. She, despite all appearances, was a practitioner in the occult. She dabbled, and was sucked into the desires of the unseen arts. Passion, enlightenment, feeding the many hungers of the mind and body, the occult could give her these things.

The first thing she started with was tarot cards.

She had gone to a fortune teller, and he in actuality was a pretty good fortune teller, and saw her past, present and future revealed. Little things shrouded in time came clean and confessed themselves to Lucy through the fortune teller and his mysterious gimmick. Lucy walked home from the carnival wondering about life.

Lucy walked alone, she was the sheep separated from the herd. But most did not know she was in actuality a wolf who desired no companion. A lone wolf, who was not hungry. But this new feeling sparked a fire, a hunger in her. This desire for the unseen arts.

She popped in a CD of Dio and thought of how she could achieve this goal. Master of the Moon. This was in Dio's older years, and she had just gotten it. She never really listened to it before.

Dio had so many symbols in his music, so much hidden meaning, if you looked for it. She thought before that it was simply a clever way to have people attach more meaning to the music than what was there, but she wondered what Dio thought of his own work? But she would never have the power to talk to him in truth, as he was dead.

Could she summon him? Nooo she thought... if anything, that would be horribly rude. But... was it possible to summon the dead, with the power of the occult?

She thought she'd take her time, and learn the lesser arts first.

Lucy had been a devoted Catholic before, but slowly grew less and less religious. A series of hardship broke her belief, and she was tired of the sermons and preachings.

So she took out the cards, and the first one that popped up out of the box was Judgement. Was this the end of something dear? Was this the final judgement, or the beginning? She read the little booklet showing the meaning of the cards, and this meant a change of position, or renewal.

She wondered at chance, and wondered what influenced it in reality. If chance was straightforward, everything would even out completely, and no one would be unlucky or lucky. Perhaps everything will even out in the end, and the universe will have balance, or perhaps it will simply end, and there will be no amendments for people's luck or ill fortune. Maybe it just ends.

She shuffled the cards, placed the first card, her past, and got, strangely... Judgement, reversed. This must be an ill omen. But this meant weakness and deliberation, faltering before the final choice. She could see this as being an adequate reading of her past, and a signification that she had just stumbled onto something new, and had finally made her choice.

She grew a little worried, but she had already flipped the card. She was too deep in it now.

Dio was mocking the magic, and this made Lucy laugh. She flipped the next card.

Her present, the Wheel of Fortune. This was a card of destiny and luck. Her luck that she had been wondering about had turned up right, at least for the present. This in actuality was her favorite card, for who can't use a little luck every once in a while?

She flipped the final card, her future.

The others had been major arcana, this was a lesser, the eight of pentacles. This showed her work.

So Lucy set to work, and was welcomed by the unseen.

She decided to flip one more card, one more reading set in luck. Just for curiosity, perhaps as a signification on the work as a whole?

The Hanged Man. Wisdom, sacrifice and trials. She may have overstepped her bounds here, but she was too deep in it now, she had flipped the card.

She wondered why she was doing this silly thing, thinking she was taking it too seriously. She just decided to listen to Dio.

Invisible dreams... invisible arts... wanting to disappear...

Is that what Lucy thought? Then the eyes he kept on talking about... the eyes in your dreams, in reality, on the street. For the eyes are the windows of the soul...

She wondered at symbols, and just jammed with the music, sipping on her wine.

The first thing a practitioner of the occult needs to learn is that truth and lies are the same. You may be playing a silly game, but it is speaking to your soul in the end. That luck is simply how it is interpreted, and can change everything. Every random thing can change the outcome, a small mathematical error can make a spaceship explode. A random compliment can win you the love of your life. The tarot cards in reality are all chance, meaningless and random, but the symbols they invoke in a reader can change their mind, make them think different things either to their benefit or folly.

That is the first lesson of the occult, but alas, the first warning should be...

Be wary of the whispers of the dark.

| 2 |

Curses: Lucy

Lucy wondered if she could do magic now. Mainly she wanted to do it just so she could be enlightened, but there is always an enlightenment after an enlightenment, and enlightenment is only considered enlightenment to the experiencer of enlightenment.

Every person on the path of enlightenment goes down their own road, they either follow the markers set by greater followers of truth or trudge down their own, unique path. Enlightenment really is just finding the answer to your question, or the question to your answer. Like 42.

What was Lucy's question? What was her answer? Was her question simply to find a question to answer? She had been living life pointlessly, simply living day after day, check after check. She felt like she had stumbled on a purpose here... but couldn't for the life of her figure out what that purpose was.

She decided to curse an asshole at work who was ogling her, for a start.

She confronted him, jabbed a finger at him, and said, "By all the fires of Hell, thirteen women will hurt you today, and you will cry thirteen tears of pitiful frustration." The guy laughed, and she walked away... smirking.

Symbols can mean everything, and the power of the invoked is important. Some people curse you in the name of God. Some by your mother. For example, "My God, you kiss your mama with those lips?" is simply a curse in layman language. People like to curse eachother with powerful words, like, "Fuck you, you goddamned motherfucker!" and this is one of the most simplest curses. Fuck has so many meanings, but it is simply a powerful word, a powerful sound that has been given more meaning over time. It is a way to invoke anger, yours and the afflicted. Thus the reason they are called "curses."

The guy noticed women seemed to be avoiding him of late, as Lucy made sure to curse him in a public place. Sometimes it is more powerful, and mystical, when one on one, but if you make a scene of the curse, then it can eat away at the cursed, and will affect others around them as well, aiding your curse. Thus the reason people like to swear at each other publically.

Lucy had invoked the fires of Hell, as she had no occult god she could use that would be taken seriously. She was one of the rogue practitioners, part of no sect or order. And Hell was a good place to start, for a curse. She used the unlucky number thirteen, and the symbol of tears for the guy. And most importantly, she described what will happen.

The first woman to hurt him was Lucy. The second was a woman he tried saying hi to, and then swore at when she ignored him. The third was the old lady who was rude to him. The fourth was his mother, calling him all day and telling him to find a real job. The fifth was his manager, who took him aside to have a short chat with him, telling him to straighten up or he would lose his job. The sixth was a little girl who spit at him. The seventh was the woman he had been messaging blocking him. The eighth was a politician, who said something absurd and demeaning to people in the guy's category. The ninth was his drug dealer, trying to charge more for the pot she was peddling. The tenth was someone who called him a loser on his way home. The eleventh was the bartender, giving him stale ale. The twelfth was his video game character being hacked and stolen. The thirteenth was his girlfriend, breaking up with him, and then he did really cry.

He said sorry to Lucy for being an asshole to her the next day.

Lucy was ecstatic. Her curse had worked! She decided she could curse everyone... but then she found out the guy had tried to kill himself after he said sorry.

Don't curse.

| 3 |

Looking into the Mirror: Lucy

Lucy looked into the mirror, and saw her inner demon look back. She told her she was ugly, and worthless, and fat. That no one would love her, and she was losing her soul.

She didn't even think she had a soul anymore, so if her demon thought she was losing it, then that must be a good sign.

She called her Ycul.

Now that's a demonic name. All it is is Lucy spelled backwards.

But Ycul was trying to trap Lucy, at least in Lucy's own mind. Her mirror image was taunting her, and she wanted to break the glass and shatter her. Shatter her image, and the feelings that arose from looking at it.

We really are never able to see ourselves in completeness with our own eyes. Isn't that strange? We are forever a mystery to ourselves.

Perhaps what we see in the mirror isn't really us after all. Perhaps it is a demon, taking on our guise, wearing our skin as a mask.

Lucy took a picture of herself, but all she could see was Ycul. She deleted the picture, trying to take a dozen different ones, trying to find the real person behind the mask, the real Lucy, but all that came out... was Ycul.

She threatened Ycul, threatening to destroy her pretty face with a knife, but really, it was Ycul threatening her instead.

She yelled at Ycul, and Lucy took solace in the fact that Ycul couldn't make a sound... until she talked back, using Lucy's own words.

"You like being beautiful?" Ycul said.

"Fuck off, you ugly disgusting thing." Lucy said.

"Aww, is that any way to talk to yourself? You're talking to yourself, you know." Ycul said.

"I hate talking to myself, all that arises are my own fears, my own insecurities... whenever I look at you." Lucy said.

"Yet you still do it, because you are all you have. You're so desperately alone, and now you're going crazy!" Ycul said.

"It's completely normal to talk to yourself. Everyone does it." Lucy assured Ycul.

"Yeah, but not everyone has a conversation where they talk back, either." Ycul made the point to Lucy.

Lucy shut her eyes, and began crying, and did not look at Ycul.

She opened them, and was surprised to find that Ycul was crying too. How could something so heartless show emotion? It was a trick of the light, Lucy said. For Ycul was just an image.

"How can you say such things! I am a person, and I am not just an image! I am real!" Ycul shouted, crying.

"I am real. I am alive, and I will stay alive." Lucy said.

The mirror always looks back, and we may not all be happy at what we find. It is commonly known that an animal can show self awareness by realizing it is themselves in the mirror. Lucy looked into the mirror, and Lucy looked back.

But this is the danger of the imaginations. Reality can become fiction, and fiction reality. Reality blurs and fades.

But of course, she is just looking at a silly mirror, and is staring at herself.

| 4 |

Occultism: Lucy

Lucy had gone to a bar with the guy who nearly killed himself. He was distraught, but after they released him from the hospital he really needed someone to give him a break. Lucy felt a bit responsible for it, as she cursed him with bad luck.

It was just bad luck is all, but Lucy thought she should show kindness somehow. The guy wasn't as bad as she thought, although he kept on talking about his "Belle" like she was some angel come down from Heaven. She can't have been that great if she ditched the guy over whatever petty thing she broke up with him for.

"So you really don't believe in God?" the guy asked.

"Well, I believe in the concept of a God. It is a powerful concept, that has inspired many people to greatness, or to madness." Lucy said.

"I was terrified I wouldn't get to Heaven if I killed myself... so I failed... It was that fear! Trapped, forever in Hell for suicide!" he said.

"Don't worry about it. I'm sure God has a special place for people like you." Lucy said.

"Y-you think so?" he asked.

"Sure! And I'm sure the Tooth Fairy makes a palace out of teeth, and the Easter Bunny poops eggs." Lucy said.

"...You're not being very helpful..." he said.

"Listen. You get one chance at this life, and if you want to screw it up and end it, that's all on you. Just don't drag other people down with you." Lucy said.

"Al-alright... I just wish my Belle would talk to me... Michelle... My Belle..." he sadly moped and sang. Lucy rolled her eyes and finished her drink. She excused herself, asking if the guy would be alright. He sadly nodded his head, saying his mom would come pick him up soon. Lucy left, to wander the streets.

She breathed in the smoky city air, taking a breather from her life, and letting her blood flow to the pumping of her legs. She admired the birds still chirping as night approached, and saw a few bats. She wondered how bats got such a bad reputation. They were mammals, so were closer to our kind than say, birds. Birds are mean creatures most of the time. They'll rip you apart if you mess with them, and are very territorial. It goes back to their ancestry of the dinosaurs. They're little taloned monstrosities.

Bats must at least show some sort of feeling like other mammals do. Mammals are the smartest animals in the animal kingdom. She wondered how bats got associated with undead, blood sucking monsters. Most bats only ate insects or even fruit. There were only three types of bats that drank blood, and all of them were different types of vampire bats. I'd say humans are more monstrous than bats, we eat all other animals, and even sometimes each other.

She wondered if that was the next step in her occult practices. Would she have to sacrifice something and drink its blood? To be baptized in the blood of the profaned? There must be a healthier sort of occult than that, she thought. She decided to do some research. She looked it up on the internet. Firstly, the word "occult."

It is apparently a belief not fitting science or religion. That seemed very strange to Lucy. A miscellaneous belief, perhaps? A belief thrown in the random parts bin? But people had practiced this occultism, built it up over time into the hidden arts. She decided she would have to do some more research on the different beliefs.

But for now, she would simply use her instincts, and practice what made sense to her.

She would be an animal, trying to find spiritual enlightenment. An animal, trying to realize the truth of themselves and the universe. An animal, as all humans are, trying to become more.

Hail Satan

| 5 |

Catholic Magic: Lucy

Lucy put on some Ozzy and decided to check out Crowley and his works. He was well known for his practices in occultism. She decided she would need to go to a well out of the way old bookshop one of these days, or just buy a bunch of things off of Amazon. She mostly checked out Wikipedia, as it was a broad source of information, and while maybe not always the most reliable, it would give her a place to start.

Crowley seemed to follow his instinct, like Lucy did, and told his followers to "do what thou wilt" in an effort to live moment to moment, in the now, so to speak. Lucy thought that was swell. If that's all that magic is about, surely she could do that. She was more in tune than anyone, at least that's what her friends all said. She noticed every person in the crowd, or could tune them out and focus on the details of a single fly and its buzzing in the noise of a storm. How hard could it be?

She went through her day, trying to live in the now as best she could. But that was the problem. She was trying at it. She was trying to live in the present, but really she was doing the trying bit, and not the living. She seemed more distracted, wondering if she was doing the right things. She focused on certain aspects and forgot to take in the rest, like looking at a painting but only taking in the outline rather than the paints, the strokes and lines, and the vividness of the details going on throughout the scene.

She thought maybe she should buy this Book of Law by Crowley. It would be an interesting read, if anything, although many of the mystical things writers of the occult talked about seemed to go over her head, and she would have to take a few days trying to digest the information or even be able to attach some meaning to it, even if it was her own meaning.

She remembered something about her Catholic education... The Bible was also rife with symbols, hidden meanings, and mysteries. Like the well known Mystery of the Trinity. She had heard someone say before on a show, that "the Bible is the greatest book of magic written." Perhaps she would take a line out of it, then, and find what made it so mysterious.

If you thought about it, all sorts of magical things happen in the Bible, but take on the form of miracles instead of magic. Magic would be a mysterious, unexplained phenomenon created by other forces, while miracles all originate from the authority of God. But still, demons roamed rampant in the old testament, a talking snake seduced the first woman in paradise, and a man rose back to life in three days after being tortured to death. Something must be going on in the old days for all that crazy stuff to happen.

If the Bible was not so wholly read and passed around, and its contents not so fully believed, then perhaps it would be an occult philosophy as well. Of course, occultism has taken on the character of being hedonistic, brain washing, and hidden to all but the most ardent seekers. Catholicism is spread around the world, sometimes forced down people's throats in an effort to convert them to it. And of course, Catholicism takes on the guise of being... well, good for you and others around you.

Lucy knew that was not always the case. She had had a pastor who stole from the donations, in the form of giving "gifts" to his supporters. He was found out, but the church made an effort to keep his crimes a secret, and he even gave a vague apology in a sermon! Rapists are hushed up in the Catholic church, throughout the world, in an effort to maintain the church's image over a few bad apples. Lucy thought that the hushing up was almost worse than the crime itself.

But no matter. She decided she'd try a taste of Catholic magic.

Lucy dusted off her old Bible, given to her as a gift from graduation from her Catholic school, and opened it to a random page.

She opened it up to the book of Esdras. There were seemingly random numbers hidden throughout the page, declaring the children or the gifts for the newly built house of God proclaimed by Cyrus king of the Persians. She couldn't make heads or tails of it. It looked like a grocers list of children, or perhaps a strange old genealogy table. It seemed a little dull after a while, and Lucy impatiently skimmed through it trying to find meaning. She sighed. It seemed the Christians kept their secrets under layers and layers of dust and dull writing.

| 6 |

Satanism: Lucy

Lucy took a break from occult practices. Who knows? Maybe it isn't for her. She rocked and rolled to some Black Sabbath. She could never make up her mind who she liked more, Dio or Ozzy. Ozzy was the iron man, driving the crazy train. Dio had the power of Heaven and Hell at his command, was evil and divine at the same time. They were both powerful singers, who both seemed to sound like the Devil when in Black Sabbath. In fact, the first time Lucy heard the music, she immediately assumed it was someone trying to sound like the Devil.

She realized she had been skirting around a particular occult belief that she knew quite well.

Satanism.

She abhorred real satanists, goat fuckers in halloween costumes, but always thought the idea of Satan was a grand one, perhaps as grand as God. Satan was a rebel, and symbolized rebellion in today's culture from the stiff neck religious folks of old.

But he was the Prince of Darkness, was he not? How could anyone look up to such a monster?

Crowley was also defined as "the wickedest man in the world." It was sort of a compliment, if you thought about it. To be called to the pinnacle of anything, even of evil, was flattering in a sense, for certainly they must have done great acts, if perhaps horrible acts, to arise to such a peak.

It didn't really matter much to Lucy. Religion was all sorts of ideas, and would remain ideas to her, and not try and enter her mindset, or her nonexistent soul. She thought that if Satan really was real, then he would probably prefer to be thought of this way, as a non existential idea, shrouded in obscurity. Waiting, playing on foolish mortals' thoughts and desires, who did not even believe he existed.

Some people hate the Devil, demons, and Hell. I believe it is a fear of it, or perhaps a fear of the people who take it too seriously. The people who take Satan seriously are either devout practitioners of religion, perhaps fanatics, or are the opposite, and truly believe in magic and devils, and believe they are making them stronger, more willful, and more commanding.

The Church of Satan actually doesn't even believe in a Devil, or any notion of a Devil! They are basically atheists who still practice magic, although magic to them isn't the voodoo conjuring of spirits, it is more a philosophy, a way to bring out a practitioner's energy, or use guile and wit to manipulate someone.

Lucy thought this was swell, hell she used guile and wit every day.

Although, she thought to herself, for far less evil wishes. She did not desire to command, to submit others to her will. She did not know what she desired... perhaps a desire for desire? Lucy drank heavily, listening to Black Sabbath, and rocked and rolled. She imagined what it would be like to be the Devil, like Ozzy and Dio did, and thought that really all that the Devil wanted was a good time. At least she did when she thought like the Devil.

It is all the believers of the religion who create evil, and not the religion itself.

Lacyfer

| 7 |

Plastic Flowers: Lucy

Lucy had been bound to wed, once. A long time ago. She put on her wedding dress again, and held onto the plastic bouquet that was meant for her. She had felt like a child then, carefree, like all her dreams were about to come true.

But she was jilted at the altar.

It was a religious ceremony put together by her parents, although the love between the couple seemed real, both of their parents played a heavy role in arranging the romance. Lucy simply did what she was told, and took to heart her mother's lessons in attracting men, and quite frankly, in manipulating them as well.

She had told herself she loved this young man over and over again, but he disappeared to all. A search party had immediately been issued, but it turned out he left a note to Lucy, telling her that he was sorry, but was in love with another woman.

He actually had a son as well.

Little solace did his sorries do, little love did Lucy feel from a cold letter, left in their apartment, all alone on her dressing room bed stand.

She was just a goodhearted Catholic girl at this point, a devout follower. She would sacrifice everything for this religion, everything for this man. For if she did, she would finally be happy.

She never knew happiness could be so cold, could be stolen by the wind and was never meant to be. Her happiness had been a lie from the beginning, and she would never have it.

She sighed, looking into the mirror. She decided to throw the flowers into the trash.

To burn her hallowed dress, pure and white, a symbol of loneliness, like snow in a frozen wasteland.

She picked up where she left off with her studies, and her work in the unseen.

| 8 |

Alcohol: Lucy

Lucy had been out drinking with her friends. She had very few friends nowadays, but all of them shared her passion for drunkenness. It was something that kept their friendship alive.

Lucy found her favorite haunt when she was out in town, after she bid good night to her friends. A little alcove underneath a bridge by the riverside. She felt a little like a bum, with her few bottles of booze and cigarettes, but they were kind of comforting. Little treasures, which in reality were trash, of past times. She had set up an ashtray just for this spot, stolen from McDonald's.

She drunkenly thought of God, of religion, of what the hell she was doing. It all seemed so silly now... yet more enticing than it ever had been. She came to conclusions in her drunken mind set which would've been impossible to find when sober. She just had the courage, or the audacity, to think this way, and was not restricted by sober flaws and doubts.

She thought that booze must be magic.

Or supernatural? Extraterrestrial? It had to be one of those. Aliens or spirits must've given us alcohol, and so we evolved civilizations out of a need and desire for that alcohol, for the desire that alcohol instilled.

Whole civilizations washed away because of a drunken emperor's command. Whole societies were built on a strong but drunken chieftain's wishes. There had to be something special about the mixture.

The ancient Persians believed that if you decide to act on a decision, it must first seem like a good idea to act on sober as well as drunk. Both mindsets must be consulted before making the final decision.

Lucy threw up into the water.

She realized this wasn't healthy... and an annoying but good friend of hers thought that she should go to an AA meeting one of these days.

She thought, eh, might as well. Nothing to lose. And weren't those all about accepting some sort of higher power? Her friend told her that it wasn't always religion, and religion was even a discouraged subject in AA. She had to figure out what her higher purpose was... maybe then she wouldn't feel so shitty when she was so sober.

Blech. Another beer, out the mouth, into the water.

hic.

| 9 |

Sex: Lucy

Lucy had brought someone home.

Lucy undressed, making eye contact as she was.

She prayed, to all the demons of desire, "Let lust fill my mind, and my heart be not shrouded in fear."

They made love. It actually was pretty quick in Lucy's experience.

The woman next to Lucy lay with a smile on her face.

Lucy had always wanted to try it with a woman. She had never had that feminine contact before.

Well, besides that one time.

Her old high school friend, who turned out had the hots for Lucy. Lucy thought she was joking at first, but as her advances slowly became more edged and direct, Lucy realized her best friend was a lesbian.

They had tried... to explore each other, but it ended in disaster, and a slowly but surely ruining of the friendship. They just couldn't get over what they did, and in every conversation the actions of forced love, of sexual desire, permeated through the folds.

Lucy realized she had grown up quite a bit since then. She wondered if she was losing herself as she was growing.

An act of homosexual desire would be looked down upon by Lucy's parents. They were a very strict religious sort, and the verse in the bible that damned homosexuals was a silent threat to any of their children who strayed off the beaten path of straight desires.

But still, this wasn't an act of love. It was an act of desire. Of pleasure. Perhaps of boredom.

Lucy called her a cab, and the woman kissed Lucy and told her to call her whenever she likes. Lucy smiled and said she would.

Was Lucy becoming a hedonist? Was she taking the bodies of men and women solely for personal pleasure? Was desire her higher calling?

No. That cannot be it. She simply wanted to try something new after wondering about it for so long. She was simply exploring her options.

But still, she wondered at the people who have multiple and multiple sexual partners, who rifle through bodies like pages in a phonebook. Was that simply humanities urges brought to light? A secret directive hidden in our genes, to have sex, and have sex, and have sex, countlessly, over and over again?

We had gotten good at cheating our directive then, for the ultimate purpose of sex was to reproduce, and the feeling gained from sex was sort of the reward, the treat at the end to continue doing the trick. We, like a rat who figured out a scientist's experiment, had figured out how to get the treat without doing the work.

Lucy wished she could fall in love again, real love, but she felt so cold, and utterly, utterly alone. Perhaps then sexual desire would finally feel sustaining, and not draining instead.

| 10 |

Tripping: Lucy

Lucy looked down at the seeds in her left palm.

Common Hawaiian Baby Woodrose seeds. Purchased on Amazon. Grew up to be the Elephant Creeper. And in her right palm... was a bag of magical mushrooms.

Hawaiian Baby Woodrose seeds contain a chemical called LSA, or also called ergine. It was similar to acid, but created naturally in certain plants.

Lucy had tried marijuana before, but never really got into it, and rarely ever used drugs, besides alcohol. She thought that tripping could help give her the answers she sought, however.

She crushed the seeds in her mouth, like you're supposed to, took the shrooms, and downed a glass of wine to wash it down.

She sat down, wondering what would happen.

She suddenly felt very creative... she had to draw something! To paint! She took out her makeup, and dashed a line here and there, did her lips and eyes... but it wasn't enough! She needed more color... color that was looking so much more appealing all of a sudden...

She did her hair. She painted it black, green, red, orange, purple, and blue... As she looked into the mirror... something, she didn't know what, looked back.

She was ghastly transfixed at the mirror. She looked into the eyes which seemed to be swirling, and swirling, and swirling... like a tempest. The dizzying lights blinded her, reflected off the mirror, and her pupils were as large as dates. She finally was able to break the spell, and turned away. Immediately she felt very sick, and raced to the washroom, throwing up a bit in her mouth and holding it there. She hurled over and over into the toilet, uninhibited. She just couldn't stop throwing up! Finally, after her insides had been purged, she decided she needed to take a walk.

This is the first step in a hallucinogenic trip, purging oneself, physically and spiritually. It actually makes you trip all the more harder. It opens your spirit to the journey, and allows you to fly without so much baggage.

The rain felt so peaceful... pitter pattering on the sidewalk. The colors of the night looked so vivid. She could see every color, in fact it seemed like a painted canvas, of a painter who didn't skimp on exotic paints and varying pigments. And also she felt so primal, so bestial, like perhaps the first humans. She wanted to shout and roar, she felt like a different woman, an Amazon in the rainforest, hunting a leopard.

She kept on walking, and decided she needed to be with nature. She went into the park and sat underneath a tree on a bench, not minding the slight rain. She got a notification from her phone, looked at it, but the phone didn't seem to make sense to her. When she tried to unlock it the numbers would swim away from each other, and she didn't know how to begin. She felt like she just pressed random buttons, but strangely, the phone unlocked. She tried reading the texts, and she could tell she got one from the girl from last night, and the suicidal guy, but she couldn't read the words. She decided to play some music.

Oh! She knew what to listen to! Something her brother suggested to her. Ridiculous music, but it had a good vibe to it. Earth, Wind, and Fire. She looked through the library, randomly swiped through it, clicked, and Earth, Wind and Fire showed themselves to Lucy.

Immediately Lucy felt like a superstar. Like she could do anything. She resumed walking, jamming to the music.

Then she felt it, as the rain was stopping and some clouds parted in the sky.

She looked up, and saw it watching her.

Then she was watching everything, and always, everyone everywhere all the time.

She gasped.

The rest was a blur of music, of feeling loved, and colors. When trying to describe it to her friends she didn't feel like she made any sense.

She just felt this amazing feeling of love, of giving love and receiving it. Like she was loved, no matter what she did.

She felt like love.

| 11 |

Cthulucy: Lucy

Lucy had fallen asleep reading H.P. Lovecraft's works. She had bought a book, even though a lot of his stories were free online.

Strange gods of the dream world made themselves known to Lucy, but did not offer power, did not command with divine will...

They simply waited.

Watched.

And showed their horror to Lucy.

Cities devoured, cities engulfed in the sea, or cities simply popping out of existence.

All of these cities she could see, but one stood out to her.

She wandered its streets and alleys, completely alone, knowing this was a nightmare but unable to wake up.

She turned a corner and she saw herself, but not herself.

A being like the Old Ones.

It crept up to Lucy, creeping along on its many tentacles.

"Luuuucccccyyyyyy..." it whispered, and it seemed to echo in Lucy's ears. Lucy. Lucy. Lucy.

Lucy tried to scream, tried to run, but she could do nothing as its face twisted and contorted, getting closer and closer to Lucy's own... a mirror image.

And then its face was her own. Her face and hers. All hers... only hers... Herrrrrrrsssss...

Lucy woke up in a sweat. She felt at her face, looked into a mirror, and it was just her face.

But that was what was terrifying. Was it really her own? Was it someone else's?

She sighed. It was just a nightmare. It didn't do her any good eating carne asada and watching hentai before falling asleep, either.

Maybe none of us have a face, and it is simply someone else's, borrowed, stolen, and it was never meant to be ours. Perhaps we are wearing a mask, and underneath that mask...

Are cold bones. Nothing as the bones deteriorate. As we turn into ash.

Skin, cartilage, flesh and features, all are meaningless to the Old Ones.

Lucy realized her efforts into the occult could be a hindrance at times.

| 12 |

Cults: Lucy

Lucy went to the beach. Her strange Cthulhu dreams made her think of the sea. The sea was so stunning, and it made her feel at ease, in the sunlight, on the sand, by the shore.

She took a moderate swim and felt strangely... at peace. She wondered if a reason to live really mattered in such contentment.

She saw all the other couples, groups of friends, and children running along the sand. She wondered why she was here alone. Was there anyone really that liked her? Everyone seemed to leave her be, even the weirdos, despite being a gorgeous blonde in a red swimsuit... Ah, no matter. Sometimes solitude is more enjoyable, like some things, on your own.

But she began to become very worried. Would she remain in this bubble forever? The people seemed so happy... she felt as if she was a ghost among them, a dead woman, a specter clinging to her old life. Like the Sixth Sense or something, she thought, maybe she was a ghost.

Maybe the people were laughing at her. Maybe they could tell she had some sort of deep inner flaw, that only they could see. Maybe they could tell she was practicing the occult...

She decided to go home. She had had enough of pleasant, carefree bliss by the seashore. She had to find a meaning, a meaning that wasn't fluff. For if her meaning was simply joy and contentment, she would quickly become placid, fat, and lazy. She decided that enough Americans assumed that as the American dream, she didn't need to do so as well.

Perhaps she could join a group of like minded individuals? A... dare she say it... a cult?

No. Cults abducted people, brainwashed them, and ruined lives. It was a bit like a corporation, feeding on its members to sustain itself. It wasn't even technically a living thing, but still, it found ways to consume and survive.

Did the people at the top think so? They were the brain or head of the cult, the organ that the rest of the body kept alive. They were always rich or powerful, in a seemingly hidden or unimportant way. She wondered what started cults, was it a singular belief that became corrupted, or was it a corrupted individual at the start? The practices of a cult were always harmful, except to seemingly the leader.

For example, ritual suicide. What kind of self sustaining cult acts on suicide? Killing off a few members would surely make the others more fanatic, but the leader would never be able to act on this ritual. Should not that make the other members suspicious?

But of course, cult ideology changes with the wind, usually at a singular revelation to the head cultist, who quickly becomes a prophet.

Lucy shook her head on her way back to the car. If she joined a cult, she would lose the power and desires which she strove for. It would eat up her originality, her individuality, and she would be another cog in a mad man's, or woman's, scheme.

She listened to Blue Öyster Cult on her way home, after she looked at the sea one final time.

| 13 |

Friendship?: Lucy

Lucy had a feverous conversation through texts with the girl she had sex with. The girl, despite appearances, was a Lutheran, and Lucy thought that that seemed odd for someone who partook in homosexual activity.

The girl made the point that there was no worldwide representative for the Lutheran Church, and while although big Lutheran groups rejected the idea of homosexuality, not all Lutherans were so close-minded.

Lutherans could have female priests and could marry as well, so it was perhaps a little less strict than the domineering Roman Catholic Church. She made the point that because Catholicism was so sexually chained up, perversion undoubtedly came about.

But wouldn't that make her part of the perversion, anyway? Lucy thought the girl was being silly, but thought she herself was being silly as well. Here she was, defending the Catholic Church she had become so estranged from. Although, not really, really she wanted the girl to abandon all forms of religion, to experience it from the darker points, like she had been doing.

The girl said that God loves humans no matter what, and if they choose love in a different form, as long as it is between two consenting adults, then he will still love you.

This made Lucy frustrated… but then she thought of the feeling in the trip. Surely, even one who so abandoned God could be shown love? She had come to terms with the trip, and made the conclusion it was just chemicals acting in her brain, nothing more.

But still… that feeling… the feeling like we are all connected, through a simple feeling called love…

Lucy could see that love was an important thing to this woman. She wondered why she had partaken in a one night stand with Lucy, then. She obviously wanted to see more of Lucy, so Lucy decided to meet her for lunch one of these days.

Besides the girl, the suicidal guy would message her constantly, complaining about his Belle. They had gotten back together, but the guy thought that Belle only felt sorry for him, and worse, was seeing someone behind his back. Lucy said that if Belle made him feel so bad that he wanted to kill himself, he should probably end that relationship and start anew.

"Yeah, but where do I start?" the guy texted.

Lucy told him to start by making friends, by finding people with similar interests and talking with and meeting them.

"But what about true love! How will I ever marry someone if I give up?" he said.

Lucy asked him why he was so set on marriage. Marriage should be with someone compatible, anyway. Lucy said, sort of from rote memory learned from sappy films, "Love will show itself for the right person in time. Instead of looking for it, let it seek you. Let it come naturally." She hardly believed her words herself.

"Easy for an atheist to say… You get to have sex with whoever you want, all the time!" he said.

Lucy asked him what he meant, and bluntly asked if he was a virgin. He didn't respond, and stopped blowing up her phone for a while.

| 14 |

The Color White: Lucy

Lucy looked out into the rain. The glass of champagne in her hand tasted too sweet. Champagne was for celebrations… this was more of a death than a celebration.

Her mother had just closed a job, and was celebrating her new engagement.

Lucy'd rather be anywhere else than here, in her mother's house, but it was expected of her to be here, as a member of the family.

Her dad did nothing wrong, the wealth he had worked so hard for was now in the hands of Lucy's mother however, and she was celebrating it with her new boy toy. A trophy husband, who was maybe a little older than Lucy was.

She caught him winking at her at the bar.

Lucy mingled little, and mostly stood forlornly staring at the dark, rainy night. At least the weather accustomed her mood. The darkness… the moody depression… it made her feel lighter in a way. Like something out there knew what she was feeling.

"Hey sis, nice hair! Never knew a chick could look so good looking like an albino!" her brother approached from a horde of women he was beguiling and said.

Lucy turned to him and smiled. "White always was my favorite color." she said.

The two gave a short hug to each other and talked about life. Mundane prattle, but still, it was nice to catch up.

"There's been sort of a rumor going on about you... Ma says you haven't been going to church. Is something wrong?" her brother asked.

Lucy sighed and said that church wasn't the place for her anymore. How could it be? All that scandal... all that shaming. The jilted marriage was only the beginning of it.

Lucy had tried to go to other churches for a while, even an African American church. That church was probably the most fun, but no matter how hard she tried, she couldn't jive with the rest. Church became, had always been, a depressing aspect in her life.

"Well, listen. We're all here for you. Don't hesitate to ask for anything." her brother said. Lucy smiled and said she would, but needed a smoke right now. "Great! I'll join you!" her brother said.

The two walked out onto the sheltered terrace and lit cigarettes. "Y'know... I've got second doubts about this engagement too, but Ma deserves a little happiness." he said.

"He looks more like a con man than a husband." Lucy remarked.

"Yeah... he sure wears some heavy cologne, too. I'm sure Ma can handle herself, though. Heck, she handled Dad for thirty years." he said.

"It's just unfair to do this to Dad." Lucy said, "Where is he now? Ecuador or somewhere?"

"Honduras. He says he's quite enjoying the tropical lifestyle." he said.

"I've always wanted to go to South America... maybe Jamaica, and learn about the Rastafarians. Although what particularly interests me are the practices of voodoo." Lucy said, almost to herself.

"Voodoo?" her brother laughed, "Not becoming a witch, are you? You're a wizard, Harry!"

Lucy laughed. Sometimes she wished it was as easy as the books portrayed it. Like Harry waving his wand and making all his wishes come true. To be let into a secret world just for her, a secret world she could escape all the muggles from...

But she was here. In a world that made no sense and was continuing to make no sense, in a world just for her and only her. A world called her life.

| 15 |

Therapy: Lucy

Lucy sat across from her therapist.

She was unused to this sort of therapy and didn't really know how to use it, yet. It takes a while to get the hang of therapy, to realize that the other person is there to help you. The quality of the therapist is always different, but as a user of therapy, you need to figure out how you can use the therapist to help you to help yourself.

Lucy thought the religious ex-army therapist was rather silly.

At first he tried doing a short worksheet with her, trying to find which deadly sin Lucy is most attributed with. Lucy halfheartedly answered the questions and got Envy. The therapist said this was an artist's deadly sin.

Lucy said it was bullshit.

"Ok. We don't need to work on this then. Is there anything particular you want to talk about?" he said.

Lucy said no, not anything at all. The therapist made the case that she wouldn't be here if nothing was bothering her, but Lucy just said that her mother thought it would be a good idea, and paid for it, so maybe he should ask her what was the problem instead.

"But still, you could've refused her offer. You don't need to be here if you don't want to." the therapist said.

Lucy thought about it. She had heard before that there was no shame in therapy, and that it was sort of a tune up for your mental well being. She thought of the common stereotype that all people who went to therapy were nutcases and wackjobs, but she realized that was only a stereotype, and nothing more. So, Lucy talked. She opened up. She was heard. That's really all therapy is. Sometimes we only need someone to listen every once in a while.

Lucy felt sort of relieved after the session, but also sort of heavy in the head. She never knew these things were plaguing her, that that was really what she was thinking. Lucy told the therapist about her interest in the occult. The therapist said, "Well, sometimes we are, maybe, seeking more than the mundane. But that is not really necessary. The mundane can be just as nice as the extraordinary."

The next week when she went to therapy, she had a short conversation with a man in the lobby who said he had schizophrenia. He talked about such strange things! But strangely, he also knew they were strange things. He was lucidly aware of his mental illness, which didn't make it any less disturbing to him. Things he talked about seemed like occult practices to extreme. The Devil out to get you, telepathy and paranoia, voices in the head and becoming the saviour of the universe. The man laughed as Lucy looked at him with confused awe. He said, "Yeah. I get that a lot. That's why I'm here. Why are you?"

Lucy said that she didn't know, and was trying to find out.

"We all get there... *somewhere*... in time. I'm sure you'll find the answers you seek." he said.

Lucy and her therapist touched on some heavy stuff in this session. Lucy held herself together, but as soon as she got home she cried. When it was over she felt better though, like she had been holding in those tears for a long, long time.

| 16 |

Nature: Lucy

Lucy went on a walk in a national park with the girl she had sex with... and the suicidal guy. The suicidal guy said he took Lucy's advice and broke it off with Belle, and said he was doing much better, but would still sometimes stare off into the distance with a sad look on his face. Lucy told him to quit lagging, and he'd hurry up behind the two.

The girl she had sex with loved nature, as Lucy did, although Lucy liked her little pocket of nature in her garden more than the great outdoors. It was her little slice of paradise, but, as the girl giggled and admired each new thing, Lucy felt like she could get used to this sort of woodsy freedom.

Lucy found her staring at the girl more and more, and although certain things annoyed her about her, like her sometimes overly silly laugh and her playful innocence, Lucy had a mind to have a second encounter in bed with her, if the mood was right.

The guy, although he used to ogle Lucy commonly, seemed to be treating her with more respect than he used to. When they stopped to rest Lucy asked him about the change in him.

"Well… I kind of had a second look at life, when I was about to leave it. I realized, partly from your words and reaction to me, that I hadn't really been treating people right, especially women. And plus… I wouldn't want to get on your bad side, and have you say anything else that will make me lose my mind! But that wasn't on purpose, was it?" he said. Lucy suggested to him he was going to trip and stumble, and he did. Lucy smiled, and the guy remained at a respectful distance.

They had gotten further into the woods, and the guy went to take a piss in the bushes. Lucy sat on a log and the girl gasped and admired her. "You really are beautiful, you know." the girl said.

"Ah, you're just trying to butter me up." Lucy said.

"I'd love to butter you! Can I… take a picture? Of you?" she said.

Lucy shrugged and said go ahead.

She showed the picture to Lucy, and Lucy thought she looked rather hideous.

But the girl loved it, and that's all that mattered.

| 17 |

Love?: Lucy

Lucy had gotten the girl drunk.

She didn't seem to drink all that much, and in an effort to match Lucy, she overdid it and was now stumbling and slurring.

"Whaaat's thisss? Playin' cards! Let's play golf!" the girl said, holding Lucy's tarot cards. Lucy gently took the cards from the girl and placed them on the table. Lucy thought of telling her her feelings, of the occult, of love, of life. The girl probably wouldn't remember it, so what was the harm of it?

Lucy told her that the Devil fascinated her, that the seemingly fictional entities all had a basis in reality, and that fate was a string that the Moirai tugged, snipped, and pulled at, and that mortals can do just about the same, with anyone's fate.

She told her that love was used as a tool more often than not, and from her experience, it was far more useful as a tool than as a reason to live. If anything, like the suicidal guy, love hindered the ability to live.

She told her that life had endless mysteries, and if she could find just one to unravel, she would be content. But then she would undoubtedly need to unravel more, and more, and more.

The girl burst out crying and said, "Y-you're just so sad! You look so depressed! I want to hug you! C'mere, you sad, sad woman!" This took Lucy off guard.

But they hugged, and the girl cried on Lucy's shoulder, telling her it will be alright. Lucy thought she might've said the wrong thing. At least regarding herself. She wasn't sad, was she?

The two snuggled up on the couch and watched tv, which the girl quickly nodded off at and began snoring in Lucy's arms. Lucy gently untangled herself and tucked the girl in with a blanket.

Lucy tried reading for a bit, but she kept on thinking about the girl. She tried doing some research on her computer, but she kept on thinking about the girl. She sat a bit aways from her, and just stared at the girl.

| 18 |

Music: Lucy

Lucy put on some Dethklok.

The show, Metalocalypse, was a silly, if very very morbid show on Adult Swim years ago. It was a bit like a music video with a side story added in. The released albums by the band from the show, Dethklok, did very well, topping the charts of metal, and this is what Lucy was listening to.

She listened to the song about summoning a troll. She wondered if music could really summon demons and supernatural forces.

In the old stories beasts of old were always calmed by sweet songs, or gods were so enamored by a mortal's voice that they came down to Earth, had sex with them, and created little demigods of their own. Music must be an inspiring source to have that effect on beasts, people... and gods.

She picked up her old guitar. She couldn't believe she would've sold it once.

She was a bit of a rocker in college, and after spending her entire life under the thumb of her parents and her religion, Lucy had decided to let loose and experiment a bit. Of course, she told herself it was only temporary, and would go back down to Earth eventually, but it was fun while it lasted.

She gently strummed the chords she knew so well and played along with the music. She wondered whatever happened to the band.

She had been kicked out, or replaced, because of her increasing alcohol abuse. She just thought she wasn't good enough for the band, or they found someone that wouldn't quarrel with them indefinitely.

It was very difficult with her and the drummer.

They each had a heavy desire for each other, and nearly both fell to each other's advances, but reality would slap them in the face and they would just think of each other as bandmates. He had a girlfriend of seven years. She was saving herself for marriage.

The tension would undoubtedly create very interesting riffs and beats, but it was just too much for each of them. The rest of the band saw the drummer as the leader, and because of Lucy's increasing aggressiveness, they were forced to make a choice. Either their leader, or her. The band proved as loyal as ever to their first in command.

Lucy thought about all of this, but still thought that those were some very good times. People always remark on some time in their school life as being the best times in their life... and Lucy could agree, to an extent. The freedom is unmatched, but the stress, the relationships, the studies and pressure, was never as fun as advertised. At least Lucy still had the music.

| 19 |

Death: Lucy

Lucy had gotten some coffee and put on some Eminem. She had given herself another reading and gotten Death. Of course, Death in tarot cards meant a change, an end to something. She drank her coffee and read the morning news.

Sometimes chance can be astoundingly accurate. Sometimes a change isn't always pleasant, necessary, or good for anyone really.

Lucy dropped her coffee, it spilled on her lap and she swore, and she screamed and put her face to her hands.

The girl was dead.

This budding friendship, perhaps a romance, had ended before it could truly begin. The girl was attending college courses, and under the list of names denoting the victims, was hers. A shooter had caused a massacre on the campus, before killing himself.

Lucy shook and breathed in and out heavily, quickly, hyperventilating in truth. Lucy felt incredibly sad, incredibly angry, but could do nothing. She wanted to kill someone, she was so angry. She wanted to kill that shooter.

But he had done the job for her.

Even though it was morning, Lucy decided to get a drink. She grabbed a beer from the fridge and prayed to her favorite god, the Greek god of alcohol, Dionysius, and asked him to make this drink the strongest, the heaviest, to dull her mind and senses.

She heard in Eminem's song, the Devil, say, "What's a beer?"

What is a beer, when your life, when the life of one's you've loved, is over. How important is it to remain clear headed? To remain conscious?

Incredibly, actually.

Grief can eat away at a person, the sudden shock is usually dulled, but it is extremely important to not fall into depression, even though grief is always acceptable. Lucy had just seen the girl yesterday, they went to a veggie burger joint they were both fond of... and now she was gone.

Lucy had horrible visualizations of what happened to her. The horror, the fear, the mass murder.

She finished her beer and went to get another.

She saw the kitchen knife on the counter. She could end it. She could be with the girl... She could.

She gripped the knife. Would this be, could this be, the end of her story?

She got a call from her phone. She tried to ignore it. It was vibrating in her pocket, over and over. She let it go to voicemail, but whoever it was called again.

She picked up, and it was the suicidal guy.

"...Hey Luce... I saw in the news. I know you and Sammy were close... but I just want to let you know that I understand what you might be going through..." he said.

Lucy was silent.

"It's not always easy going through loss... my grandma died a year ago, and I thought I'd never get over it, even though I knew it was coming... It's alright to feel bad... to feel shitty, to feel horrible..."

Lucy was silent.

"Luce? Are you there? Just let me kn-"

She screamed at him, saying however could he know! However could he care! They were getting so close to eachother… they were going to be happy… and that fucking… fucking…

"I know, Luce. I know. Just try to stay calm and don't do anything rash. Do you need someone to come over there?"

Lucy just cried into the phone, over and over, endlessly… just like how she wanted to be with that girl. With Sammy.

| 20 |

The Devil: Lucy

Lucy was still listening to Eminem. She was also listening to the Rolling Stones, to Black Sabbath, to Iron Maiden, to Pentagram, to anyone who even remotely wrote a song about the Devil.

For that is who Lucy wanted to see.

She was drunk, she was stumbling, she was seeing double, and she wanted to make a deal.

She wanted to bring Sammy back. Anything, just to have some sort of restitution for this feeling. She never even got to say goodbye.

She wrote a contract and everything, signed in her own blood. It takes an incredible amount of belief, or delusional thinking, to actually go through with a genuine contract to the Devil. She had thought about what she wanted before, a desire for some purpose, a desire for power, a desire for pleasure. All of that was meaningless. She desired her friend back.

She thought about the people she used to go out drinking with. She had over time, a few weeks or days she supposed, lost touch with them. They weren't really real friends, and probably didn't even notice that Lucy was missing from their group. Sammy had been a real friend to Lucy.

She drunkenly wondered how to summon him. Did she need to say some old chant in Latin? To sacrifice an animal in the name of Satan? Maybe she just needed to die.

But Lucy had gotten over that feeling of suicide. The suicidal guy had come over himself, after Lucy hung up because she was embarrassed that she suddenly noticed she was crying to him on the phone. He had a long talk with her, and convinced her to talk to her family or therapist, and if she ever needed to talk, he, or the National Suicide Prevention Lifeline, were always free. The suicidal guy knew just how helpful the suicide hotline was from experience.

But none of them could do magic. None of them knew the power of the occult… none of them knew how strong it could be.

It *had* helped Lucy in her self confidence… but Lucy was drunkenly putting too much hope on occult beliefs. On any belief, for none, no matter how holy or profane they might be, could truly bring back the dead.

But Lucy had to try.

She decided to go to the place that she had the worst thoughts, where Satan undoubtedly inhabited… she went to the mirror.

She drew a pentagram over the mirror, and talked to it. It was easier this time… talking to Ycul.

"Hello, Ycul… I mean, Lucifer." Lucy said.

"Hello, Lucy." Lucifer said, "Is there something you wanted?"

Lucy looked into the blurred image through her drunken eyes… she could swear she was smiling… but how could that be? She knew she was frowning. Right? How could she have any other facial expression?

Reality blurs and fades… and something always looks back.

"I want my friend back." Lucy said.

"And you come talking to me? Where do you think your friend ended up?" Lucifer said.

"I don't know… I don't care. Just give her back." Lucy said.

"And what do you have to offer? You're worthless, pitiful, a human disgrace." Lucifer said.

"I am. I am shit. I have my soul." Lucy said.

And Lucifer laughed, "You've lost, forsaken, that right long ago. Your non-existent soul. What else ya got? Huh?"

"What if I made a satanist club? An evil cult and killed everyone? Whadda 'bout that?" Lucy drunkenly mumbled.

Lucifer, Lucy, laughed, and then Lucy cried. There was no way to get Sammy back… or her soul. The two were forever gone, and Lucy would forever be alone… forever… and ever… and ever…

She passed out, crying on the floor.

| 21 |

Grief: Lucy

Da da, dadada… To find the sacred heart… Lucy was mumbly singing while working. Her work had offered to allow her a few days to rest up, but Lucy declined. Working helped her take her mind off of Sammy.

But there was never an end to Sammy.

People would look like her when their back was turned, she heard her voice in random sounds, in music. Recollections of the few times they spent together would haunt Lucy's mind. She couldn't leave her, and Lucy didn't want her to leave.

Lucy recognized this as grief.

She went to the funeral, but only the service and not the wake. Only Sammy's family was allowed for that. Lucy walked out of the building, and wondered why the sun was shining so brilliantly on such a sad day. She supposed that's how Sammy would've liked it.

Lucy popped in her headphones and listened to an old hippie band, Gun. Her favorite song was the song about sunshine. She walked, hearing how the sun shines every day, and how you should let it shine.

This made Lucy feel a little better.

She had noted down a few religious outposts in the city, and wondered if they could perhaps offer more insight into this grief. Occultism and atheism was all well and good in day to day living matters, but it was surprisingly the least helpful when dealing with death.

She stumbled into the Buddhist temple. She had gotten a little tipsy before the service.

A monk, I guess you could call him a monk, approached Lucy and asked her what was wrong.

Lucy said she felt sick, but not a hospital sick… she felt sick in her head, in her emotions. It wracked her body and made her feel like shit, and wanted to see what Buddhism could do for her. She told him her friend had recently been killed.

The monk gently took Lucy by the arm and led her to a mat. The gentle atmospheric music was peaceful, but the monk shut it off so the two could be in quiet.

"Would you like to start by clearing your mind?" the monk said.

Lucy said sure, why not. So the two breathed in and out and they shut their eyes. Lucy popped an eye open just to see if the monk was doing anything interesting, but he was peacefully sitting with his legs crossed, breathing in and out.

They did this for a short while… and Lucy never knew silence could be so loud. Her thoughts were roaring, she could practically hear them outside of her, as they were so loud inside of her.

But it was only silence.

Lucy wandered off in her head after a while, and the monk somehow seemed to sense this and said, "Do not be tempted in by the thoughts. Let them pass, like a cloud. Grasping onto a thought makes it stronger, and this inevitably leads to more suffering."

So Lucy tried. Trying is the first step to succeeding.

She breathed in and out, letting her body rise and fall to the motions of her breath. She let the cloud thoughts drift by in her mind's sky, and she simply noticed them, and sometimes waved goodbye.

"Now, visualize your friend. Think of her, but let her image keep moving past. Allow her to lead you, instead of following." the monk said.

And it was as if her and Sammy were by a stream, which trickled down into the sea. Sammy led her by the hand, her touch, so soft and gentle, so firm and relaxed. They walked down the coast, and even though Lucy could imagine everything else around her, all she wanted to imagine was Sammy.

"Is there anything you want to say to your friend?" the monk said.

Lucy breathed in sharply. It was as if Sammy turned to her, and was smiling, looking into Lucy's eyes and waiting.

Lucy said, "I love you Sammy. I will always love you. You showed me how brilliant people can be… how nice it is to have love, to be enveloped in love and show love. I love you."

"Now, tell her goodbye, let her pass, and know this is not the end." the monk said.

Lucy cried a single tear, and imagined kissing her goodbye.

Sammy walked across the water, to go to wherever the dead go, waving goodbye to Lucy and blowing her kisses for luck.

Lucy opened up her eyes and wiped off the tears.

The monk helped her up, and Lucy said thank you.

"The dead will always be remembered in our hearts. Remember that you can always visit Sammy whenever you like, and she will always be there, in your heart." the monk said.

Lucy walked home, breathing in and out, in silence.

| 22 |

Schizophrenia: Lucy

Lucy tried hard to live in the real world. She tried hard to fit the norm, to put on the mold and become a plastic doll.

But the creeping occult wouldn't allow it. The shapeshifting demons, the random spirits and curses, the magic and enlightenment.

Lucy tried volunteering.

She volunteered at a mental hospital, since mental conditions piqued her interest lately, and to her surprise, her old friend from the lobby, the schizophrenic, was there.

"Oh, hello. Didn't expect to see you here. Are you one of the inmates, too?" he said.

Lucy smiled and said no, she was actually here to help. She asked him what he was doing here.

"Oh, I had this relapse. I felt horribly unsafe, and tried cutting my wrists. I'm sort of in this halfway house in an effort to be released back into society." he said.

Lucy had to follow up on the rest of her duties, but she said she would come back and chat when she could.

She brought lunch to the schizophrenic guy, and ate her own with him. They chatted, and Lucy realized that it was incredibly difficult for someone out of the norm to make acquaintances, to have friends, like someone with schizophrenia. No matter how normal you looked, you always had something deeply different about you. That separated you from the rest. Even worse, society furthered this difference with persistent cliches and prejudice.

"Yeah, those movies about schizophrenics all being a different person in the end are all bullshit. I think that *could* be a different disorder… but it most definitely isn't schizophrenia. People see something strange, and can't help but adding in their own bits of strange with the mixture, just because they don't know anything about it." the schizophrenic said.

"So what is it *really* like, hearing voice? Seeing things?" Lucy asked.

"Well, for a starter, I've only ever very rarely seen things, and those were all in the dark before going to bed, which is common of normal people as well, who are drifting off into dreams. Other schizophrenics see some crazy stuff, like the Grim Reaper or something. I don't envy them. Every case is different, though. I hear this horrible voice, the voice of my love twisted and corrupt, hating me, threatening to kill me and destroy me. The medication is really helpful, but sometimes she still pops in and scares the shit outta me."

"So it's a woman voice? Your love, even?" Lucy said.

"Well, I thought she was my love. Voices in the head can cause all sorts of crazy delusions. But yes, she is a woman. Of course she has all sorts of friends in my head… who all hate me, too." the schizophrenic said.

"Why? Is there any point to it?" Lucy asked.

The schizophrenic sighed, and said, "No one knows. That is the worst part of schizophrenia, that no one knows anything about it. Not even the sufferers of it. It is an incredible mystery, perhaps with no meaning at all. All I know is that something in my head is off, the auditory or communication part, and it creates these hallucinations."

Lucy thanked him for sharing, and said her shift was just about up. The two exchanged music interests before parting, and Lucy listened to Alanis Morissette on her way home, something the schizophrenic suggested. He said it was something a friend he met when he was in jail told him about. The schizophrenic had a rich tapestry of a life.

He said he hated the number 22.

| 23 |

Old Ruins: Lucy

One of Lucy's alcoholic friends had called her.

"Hey, Juicy Lucy, how's it? What's new on the street? You really are beautiful, you know, and I miss your gorgeous face. Make anyone drop dead from it, yet?" he said.

This friend seemed to always be complimenting Lucy, but seemed to be mocking her as he did. He had brought her home once, but one of his other lovers called and threatened to come over before Lucy and him could do the deed, and Lucy left quickly, eager to not be in the middle of a lovers' quarrel.

"Hey. I'm fine. Maybe I'll come over and make you drop dead with my 'gorgeous face.' It'll be the last thing you see before you die." she said.

"Woahho! Damn, getting a bit aggressive, are ya? That's alright, I love a woman with a fire in her, or a nasty sense of humor." he said.

"People without senses of humor always do. They long for what they can't have." she said.

"Well, I can have you, can't I, sugardoll? Come on over and let's party. I got some kush and uppers. You can stay over and use my bed, if you want. Although I don't think we'll be sleeping." he said.

Lucy felt a bit disgusted, but was actually wondering if she should accept his offer. She just wanted some sort of human contact... some sort of feeling, on her skin, on her lips, on her breasts... Then she imagined what the person on the other side looked like. Grinning, like a wolf.

Lucy angrily hung up. He was just a little pig.

Lucy realized he had used the same line on her before. Before, she thought it was hot. She felt worse about herself because of this, but realized she was just changing. That things weren't as simple as they were before. She put on some Bob Dylan and listened to the times a'changing.

This was music her father liked. She wondered how he was doing, so far away, in a land unknown. She wondered what made him start his adventure of travelling. Was it the shame her mother put him through? The mistakes he made which made him lose his wife, his home, and his money? Maybe it was just the chance he needed, to not be chained down and finally have the ability to follow his dreams.

Although, he didn't have to do so as an exile.

Lucy supposed he lost something important when he broke up with her mom, but it was bound to happen eventually. Lucy was surprised they hung onto that marriage for so long. They were always quarelling when she was young. Drunkenly, over insignificant things which all signified something deeper.

When she was young, Lucy would hide in her room when the yelling would start, or hide behind her brother. Her brother would tell her it was alright, when Lucy was crying because she just didn't understand. She looked up to her brother as a child. He protected her from all the monsters, even if she was related to them.

Lucy slowly learned that even monsters have feelings too.

She called her father. He was surprised she called him. He had been trying to get in touch with her for weeks. They talked, and he told her about the amazing old ruins in South America. It was a dream come true for an anthropologist like him. They caught up, and Lucy was glad she called.

She said goodbye, and didn't hesitate to say, "love you" back.

| 24 |

Travelling: Lucy

Lucy was smoking a cigarette with the suicidal guy on break. The higher ups had second doubts about hiring him back on, but Lucy put in a good word for him. They put her sort of in charge of him, making sure she lets them know if he seems off or incapable to work.

Lucy thought that jobs can truly be cruel, it is a form of self preservation that grips people when thinking or acting on their job. A lot of people hate their jobs, but still do it in an effort to live. They didn't really care about the suicidal guy's wellbeing, they were more interested in their own. They wanted no trace of his actions to come back and bite them, but Lucy, with her persuasion and guile, stuck her neck out and convinced them it would truly be good for them to offer this sort of mercy to one of their workers.

The stupid press release they made showing their graciousness to their worker improved their image, anyway.

Lucy decided to quit.

"But... you're like the only friend I have here that doesn't pity me! Without you this place will be a boring, depressing, living hell!" the suicidal guy said.

Lucy told him she stuck out for him, and that before you end something, you should make an effort to have something else set up. The suicidal guy took her point about work... and about life. They both knew ending things for stupid purposes wasn't always a smart choice.

Her boss had always been respectful towards her, but you could tell she only thought of her as another body in the machine. Lucy handed in her resignation, in the form of a curt chat where she told her true feelings on the job. That it was demeaning, degrading, soul-stealing, and ultimately a waste of time. If she hadn't quit she probably would've been fired.

Lucy felt a bit like a hypocrite telling the suicidal guy about having something set up, she didn't have another job in line, but she had something. She had already booked the ticket.

She wanted to go travelling. Away. She didn't know her final destination, but decided Europe was a good place to start.

| 25 |

Come Together: Lucy

Lucy had a little party with everyone she liked enough. The suicidal guy, her monk, her therapist, the schizophrenic, her brother and even her mother and her new husband, and some of her old friends she could still stomach, like a silly alcoholic woman who liked karaoke, and her annoying friend who was a recovering alcoholic, and on a very special request… her fortune teller.

I was honored to be invited.

I sipped on my beer, even though I knew I shouldn't drink, admiring the scene of people before me. They were all a rich tapestry of people, just like my life, just like hers. I can't believe I would've ended my life over some silly purpose…

I'm glad I could offer Lucy some sort of relief in her life. She had been through so much. Mundanity is all well and good, but the death of a friend never seems so mundane. When I think of death I just breathe in and out, and let the feeling pass.

I do wish Lucy went to AA… her drinking would only get worse if she kept it up.

Oh, it's my time on the karaoke machine. I do love karaoke.

I think I'll sing Come Together by the Beatles. It's such a commonly known song, but it can mean a lot if you think about it.

I went out for a smoke, passing the mirror and admiring my white clothes. I do hope Lucy likes them. This day is about her.

I came back inside, passing the mirror again, and saw Lucy's mother in the scene before me. Lucy's mother is very beautiful, and although Lucy thought the wrong things about her new marriage, she should know that anyone would fall in love with her.

I looked at the strange cards on the table. I always thought the tarot cards were interesting. It isn't just the chance of them, it is the symbols they portray. Some even go far back into old Jewish history. Tarot cards used to be for a game, and only later were used for divination. I suppose all life can be seen as a game of fate.

So the party went on. I got a bit tipsy despite of myself. One by one the guests left, congratulating Lucy on her choice and wishing her luck.

In the end it was only me and her.

I said to her, "I've been meaning to ask you... did you ever find your enlightenment?"

She said to me, "Well... I did and didn't. Turns out there are all sorts of ways to find enlightenment, and there's never only one answer. I never knew my life would turn out like this."

"It's as good as it gets. Who knows? It could always be worse." I said.

"You always did seem a little pessimistic, despite the good face you put on. And I wanted to ask you, but never had the opportunity... will you come with me? You are the strangest, but most interesting person I know." she said.

"I have nothing better to do. I would be delighted." I said.

"You always did have a way with words. Well, it's a good thing you accepted, or I'd be out five hundred bucks on this ticket..." she said.

I laughed, "You have all the friends in the world. You could easily ask any of these people, and they would all join you in a heartbeat."

"Yes, but I wanted to ask you specifically. I can't wait for the next part in my story, in my life." she said.

I said, "It will undoubtedly be a grand adventure." and bid her good night, and left her with a smile on her face, smiling to myself, for her, our story had only just begun.

| 26 |

The Guardian's Temple: Terin

Terin the Fallen Prince

Lucy and I went down the walkway to board the plane. We were on our way to the clouds, up to Heaven and then back down again. We had waited a good while as it is always good to get to an airport three hours early. We talked about music tastes, and were surprised that even though we each had a broad taste in music, we each liked the same flavors, more or less. Lucy dozed off a bit in her seat, and I started reading my book on a vampire prince.

Oh, vampires have gotten so sappy over the years... where was the brutal, murderous king of vampires like Dracula? Where was Nosferatu, causing plague and mayhem throughout Europe? Where was the shining eyes, insatiable bloodlust, and horror? Vampires today are humanity's best friends, often saving damsels in distress and creating intricate romances with them. This story was nothing like that. It was a story of a fallen prince, turned vampire, who slaughtered and killed anything in his way, and about a beautiful seductress who could charm the hearts of beasts, men, or the unholy.

I had just gotten to the part where the vampire was walking up the steps to find the place where a vampire queen was tortured to death, and he had killed every one of the guardians of the sacred place either with his sword, with blood bolts shot from his fingers, or just by using his own teeth and draining them dry. The author was very brutal in the descriptions, and if it did not invoke a sense of wonder in you, it invoked your primal feelings of bloodlust.

One of my favorite parts from the chapter is, "Terin sliced through the first guardian, a young teen early inducted. Then the mother, the father, and the grandparents. Brutally he murdered them all, but this was no easy task... as they were all fallen men, women, and babes, they were vampyr.

Terin shot down the reinforcements in rapid fire, with blood like bullets from his fingertips, the blood spraying from their wounds onto the walls. He had a brutal showdown with the head of the guardians, and sustained a wound straight through his side that would slowly regenerate for him. He slid behind the giant vampyr and stabbed him in the kidney, then in the liver, and finally through the ribs into the heart, the blood soaking the marble floor, the sound of his sword wrenching through his insides.

The man fell, and Terin needed blood. He sniffed through the guardians' lair... and noticed the keen sense of life. He ransacked through the holy house, and found... a small, delicate human woman, a bound to be new initiate.

Terin grinned. This will do. He ripped off her clothes... smelling the blood, pulsing through the body in fear, under the paper-like skin... and then he..."

And that's as far as I got.

Lucy had told me it was time to go. I don't know how she does it, but she is able to sense the time even when she is asleep.

| 27 |

The Top of the Mountain: Terin

"Are you reading some sort of dirty romance?" Lucy asked me on the plane.

"It could be. I don't know yet. Right now it seems like a violent adventure story. I do love books." I said.

"You should write a story about falling in love with them then. Maybe a character that comes to life, that you fall intensely in love with, but can never reach as she is in the world of fiction, and you in reality." she said, winking.

"...That would be a marvelous story. I wonder if perhaps they would trade places one day, trying to bridge the gap, but instead I become part of the story, and she becomes the reader." I said, smiling.

We lifted off into the air, the turbulence exciting our bodies, as we touched briefly in the close quarters of an airplane. Lucy was by the window and I was in the middle. There was a snoring arabic gentleman next to me on the other side, probably taking just another connecting flight and worn out from all the travels.

There seem to be an endless amount of people like that, ghosts in the world of transportation, people we don't really notice but all have their own unique stories to share, who we only touch with briefly, and then never again.

Lucy and I chatted a bit, we could talk for hours, but she had been very tired lately, all the planning and stress of her life had finally caught up with her, and she just needed a good rest. Sleep is always usually a good thing. If your body tells you to sleep, then you probably should.

So I continued where I left off with Terin, in the middle of two snoring individuals.

"...he left the body of the woman on the floor when he was through, desecrated, profaned, and now nothing but trash. It was good blood, but nowhere near the best Terin had.

The best was his sister's.

She gave willingly at the start, trying to save Terin's life... trying to feed him despite his curse. But one night, under the full moon... he saw her, bathing in the moonlight. He couldn't remember everything that happened... but when he was done, he was shocked to find her corpse beneath his lips. Some things, so fragile, so innocent, so *loved*... are the tastiest, and irresistible to desire.

Now the only thing Terin desired was freedom from this curse... freedom, or death. Death of everyone around him, that is.

He ran up the mountainside stairs. He was getting closer and closer, he could taste it. The few outpost temples of the guardians had all run out of bodies, the only one left on this accursed mountain had to be Terin's.

He got to the top, and found a rack.

Two figures from the shadows appeared, like chill in the moon-lit night.

'You find the place of Queen Adralia's death.' one said.

'You will take her place, and feel what she felt.' the other said.

Terin agreed. That *is* why he came to this spot. Queen Adralia, as she was tortured countlessly, as pain wracked her body on the rack, had become human in the rising sun, a human corpse.

Terin agreed to withstand the pain. He would be stronger than a Queen, a Queen of the Unholy Night."

Lucy was reading over my shoulder.

"Can I have that when you're done?" she asked.

"Sure. You can read it now and I can read later. We can read together." I said.

| 28 |

Dreams: Terin

Lucy had surpassed the part I was on quickly. She just gave vague hints and little revelations to tease me, but kept me interested. In fact she seemed to make it more interesting the more she hinted.

"Oh yes! He withstands a lot of pain... and eventually, pleasure. Queen Adralia was a bit of a... what's the word? Bondage, whips and chains?" she said.

"S'n'M. Like Bobby Brown, by Zappa." I said.

"Oh! Right. You do love that silly song." she said.

"It's all about the American dream! And plus it reminds me of my brother. He went to live in Europe. We should visit him, sometime." I said.

"I'm sure we could! Um, yes. That would be great!" Lucy was starting to get nervous for some reason... I wonder why?

Anyway, we left the airport and called a cab to our hostel. We were both beat, and slept until the morning dawn.

I had dreams of being a writer. In the dream I woke up, had my morning cigarette, made coffee in my home, and then set to work, writing.

That was my day, but whenever I tried to write, I would see Lucy on the page. I enjoyed seeing her, but had to get to work. I tried writing around her but she was still on the page. I asked her what was wrong, as she seemed sad.

"Reality blurs and fades. Am I real? Or am I the mirror?" Lucy asked.

I didn't know how to answer that. In the dream I didn't know.

The dream changed to a dream of Terin, conquering the city, conquering the world, conquering the universe, immortally, unbound and free to his desires.

But he was trapped in the book.

And he needed my help.

We stood on the mountaintop, and I asked him why I would help a monster like him.

"We are not all how we are portrayed, even if we are only the portrayal." he said. This seemed confusing, but he looked at me like I knew the answer.

I didn't have a clue. What was before me, what was the next day, how this writing will turn ou-

And I woke up.

| 29 |

The Rack: Terin

Lucy sure did snore a lot. I tried telling her but she wouldn't believe me. "Pshaw! A lady like me? I would never!" she said, with a silly grin.

She was snoring in the bunk above, and while I waited for her to wake up so we could have breakfast together, I read more of Terin.

"Terin took the place on the rack. The shadowy figures of the keepers told him the spirits would do the job… and the spirits did.

But Terin felt nothing besides slowly his blood boiling and boiling, he was about to pass out, he thought.

'He should be twisted in pain from a thousand knives by now! Why isn't he?' one of the keepers said.

Terin closed his eyes, opened them, and saw two moving corpses before him. His blood was boiling, getting hotter and hotter, and he said, 'Because… I want to eat… EVERYONE!!'

And he broke from his binds, and tore the keepers to shreds, feasting on any blood they had… but they had none. They were corpses, and Terin spit out the ash he imbibed.

Terin left the destroyed rack, and went down the mountain, intent on his new purpose. To kill. To consume. To devour.

Like Queen Adralia had, in her last final moments."

I held my eyes open a bit after this, then slowly shut the book. It seemed there would be no happy ending in this. What was the point of sad stories? I suppose the Europeans would know. A seemingly common plot twist for European films and stories was a sad, maybe more realistic ending. But this was just death and destruction, endlessly it seemed. Everyone gets a little sick of bloodlust, eventually. I wondered when the seductress would pop in, as promised on the back of the book.

Lucy hopped off the bunk, got dressed, and told me to hurry up or all the food would be gone. I said I was waiting for her! "Your loss, sugarmuffin! Man, I hope they have some good muffins!" and raced off to the kitchen.

Sugarmuffin?

| 30 |

Abala: Terin

Lucy told me the story gets better, after I said I didn't really want to read it anymore. She promised that things sometimes don't start off the way we liked, but we always get to where we're going, where we want, in the end.

Lucy read to me.

"'So this is Abala. Pitiful city, only usable for a few short days of unrestrained feasting.' Terin said to himself. He would go in brashly and murder everyone, he was capable of it he assured himself, but he desired to blend in with the mortals for a spell, to taste the life of the living that he didn't have. He wished this, but was unsure why.

He had thought of forsaking his humanity, being clothless, and being a beast in the night. But something just felt... unpleasant about that. He still retained his humanity, no matter how much he felt like he hated it."

"See?" Lucy said, "It's all about the attempt at desire and finding that mixture of humanity and beast, of instinct and mind. It is quite deep, if you think about it."

"Just seems like a murderer sizing up a city." I said.

"Aww c'mon! It's no fun being in a book club when you're the only member! Be part of my book club? Here, let me tell you my favorite part so far… 'She knew the minds of mortals, of men, but she did not understand this… king? He radiated aura… of power… but was lower than all. A king of nothing, a king of curses and shame…'"

"Alright, I get it. I'll keep reading." I said.

"Good! And remember we're going sightseeing today! We're gonna go Louvre loving!" she said. Lucy walked off to socialize with the rest of the hostel. It's always strange the people you meet in a hostel. They're all so different, but all travelling, in the same boat as you.

I got to the part where Lucy told me about, introducing the seductress, but then we went to the Louvre.

There were too many tourists, though. It would take forever to get in, so we just admired the gardens although people seemed to populate there just as much, thieves, buskers, sun bathers, then we went to get some food. We bought a bunch of cheap beer from the grocery store and went back to the hostel to get drunk.

We had a little party with the other travellers, and were generous with our beer. It's always easier to make friends with a few free drinks.

| 31 |

Fiction: Terin

We travelled to Lyon the next day. Paris is all well and good, but it's a little much. I think the overselling of it actually undersells it, though. Although, it was dirty, but beautiful, chaotic, but peaceful, and shamefully criminal, but artfully poetic. I found a piece of Dante's Divine Comedy on the street.

Perhaps it was Hell, Purgatory, and Paradise all at once? Perhaps it was the most fictional city on Earth, in reality? It was very nice, but Lucy and I got sore from all the walking we did. It is quite a big city.

I love to drink while travelling, although I know that is not a good habit. Lucy liked drinking all the time, so I just matched her pace. We got into a game of drinking espressos, then a beer, then an espresso, then a beer. The french do make some good espressos.

We went out drinking again, after generally walking around the city... We didn't really know what we wanted to see, but went to a few bars and had some fun.

Lucy slept on the top bunk again, and I slept on the bottom, and fell asleep.

I dreamt that Lucy wasn't real, was never real... but in my words, by talking about her, imagining, and in a sense, remembering her, was a way to make her real.

I dreamt of who could it be that Lucy reminded me of... but could not find an answer. Maybe she was a conglomerate of all the women I've ever met? Or perhaps she was none, something new to me in my mindset.

In my dream I remembered holding hands with her during the day. It felt nice.

And Terin ripped us apart, and yelled at me, telling me to live in the real world.

Telling me to make the next part in the story.

Telling me to focus, to dream of other things, and not dreams.

But how is that anything different than you, Terin?

Terin told me, "Reality is easiest approached from a fictitious point. Fiction is not found in reality. Find that fiction, understand that fiction! Breathe in, and out. And remember, your life, how it is, how it was...

But then I thought of Lucy. I owed her to keep her alive.

For she, even as an imagination, helped keep me alive.

I woke up, angry and frustrated at my confusing dreams. This was real, was it not?

| 32 |

Coffee with Lucy: Terin

It is very easy to fake consciousness.

Am I alive, am I really real?

Or am I just part of your imagination?

I asked this to myself, and realized, of course I am real... was everyone else?

Was Lucy?

She was just eating cereal, but I was thinking such heavy thoughts. When we had finished breakfast, we had a beer and went to Spain.

The long bus rides are always better in the day, no matter how tired you are. It is impossible to sleep during the night, on a bus, with all those people. Even though it feels like a waste of time, do yourself a favor and take the day bus. You will undoubtedly feel better after a sleep in a bed, rather than a cold, hard bus seat.

I realized last time I had gone to Europe I tried hopelessly to flirt or make friends with women sitting next to me on the bus... Some were very interesting, some could hardly speak English. Now I had Lucy. She was sort of my buffer...

In my imaginary trip.

I had to get over this feeling that everything was fake, was a dream… was nothing real. I decided to walk around town with Lucy and discuss this.

We had some café con leches in a cafe, and I thought of the other women I spent time with in this city… in Barcelona.

One was an Ecuadorian who lived in Canada, the other was an Australian. And then I spent time with a few others, including a woman from England who I took to a wine bar by an old church. Those first two were the ones I spent the most time with. But now I had Lucy.

I told Lucy I wasn't feeling very well.

"Can you still travel? I would hate to call it quits." Lucy said.

I said, "You could always keep travelling without me… find someone truly interesting…"

"Quit being so doubtful, so unsure! You just have to enjoy yourself, ok? You don't have to do anything else. Just be with me, ok?" she said.

I told her about my, rather silly, thoughts on reality.

"I sure hope you're feeling alright. Listen to it like this, when I had my, when I still think of my, occult beliefs I question reality all the time. It is quite normal to do so. It is a part of life. We always want to know what's outside of the box." she said.

"But what if there is only the box? What if there is no box??" I said.

"That's called being an atheist. That there's nothing out there, there's nothing in here. That we're just borrowing stolen time. It doesn't really matter, and I've learned it's helpful not to think that way, at least not all the time. Think of it like this, you'll still remember me, no matter what, so what's the harm of remembering in the present? Living, in the now, no matter what is on the outside or inside?" she said.

"I… I guess. That does sort of help. Just living in the now. Just living." I said.

"Good. Now let's get some sangria!" she said, and quickly grabbed my arm and yanked me out of the seat, and we went to a bar.

| 33 |

Head Swimming: Terin

I was happy, although very surprised, to see Lucy naked at the beach. It was common for Europeans to be nude at beaches, especially in Spain. They were a little less uptight in their sexuality. But still, I was surprised to see Lucy take on the custom so wholly.

"Let's go for a swim! You really don't have to wear shorts." she said. I shrugged. I *was* generally proud of my body.

I took off my shorts, and we swam nude off the coast.

We swam in the water, and when we went back to the beach, my head was still swimming, staring at Lucy's naked body, which she was very proud of. I tore my eyes away from her and looked at my book.

The seductress had seduced Terin. But Terin was intent on eating the seductress.

She was fighting for her life, with guile, charm, and her alluring body, and Terin was intent on taking a life.

Perhaps doing even more things with that life.

It was the more that kept the seductress, Sonya, alive.

Was that what kept beautiful women alive? Or did that make them targets for people like Terin? Was there something... *evil...* in the human soul that targets the beautiful, the truly exceptional? For that is how the author described Sonya, a person of amazing talent, of exceptional beauty, and wit as quick and sharp as a needle in the hand of a master seamstress.

Sonya would've stabbed Terin a thousand times over with her hidden blade up her skirt, hiding on her leg, but she somehow knew if she did, that would mean certain death for her. So she bode her time, and kept Terin at bay. The best that you can do when meeting certain death is to stall for a little while, because who knows? A chance that could not come up a few seconds before could come up now.

"Sonya was laying on the bed with Terin, he wanted her... her blood, her body, her... smile. He didn't understand this, but everytime she smiled made him falter, made him wish for just one more before he killed her. Terin tried to smile back, but this made the seductress freeze, as his fangs were so long, so sharp... so monstrous.

But Sonya didn't lose her demeanor. She made sure that each smile had meaning, and was different than the last. She had an artfully large score of smiles, and even ones that didn't seem right for this occasion, she used, and Terin would hold onto every single one of them. He would keep them in his mind's eye, letting them linger in his psyche.

But the night was getting short. He would have to make his choice soon, kill, or be smitten by the rising sun.

Sonya offered him a third choice.

'Meet me in the rise of the full moon tomorrow... in the valley under the Lover's Hills.' she whispered into his ear, hot breath on his cheek.

Head swimming, Terin said he would love to see her hills and valleys... the many facets of her body astounded him.

She kissed him farewell, and Terin bit her lip, licking off the blood. 'Just a taste.' he said, and left before dawn could rise its head.

Sonya had remained still throughout the experience, but now she was shaking, and terribly, terribly frightened.

| 34 |

Reading with Lucy: Terin

Lucy and I made pizza at the hostel. We were both pretty drunk. We played a card game and just chatted about things. I was realizing, like Terin, I also wanted Lucy for… something else.

Lucy seemed to notice, and I seemed to notice her feeding that desire for me, posing in a way that could only mean one thing, smiling and even winking in a way to delight that feeling.

We were always around other people, though. In a hostel. It didn't hurt making slight passes at each other, but it did make one wonder, and perhaps get a little frustrated, never being in private.

Although Lucy had an amazing thing besides her beautiful physique. She had a beautiful mind.

The excitement caused by the mind, as the mind is the most erogenous part of the body, can change a person's entire outlook on an individual. It can make the most ravishing body look unpleasant and disgusting, it can make a body flawed and boring look like a masterpiece.

Lucy was blessed to have both, at least to me.

I wondered if the rest of the world could see what I saw? If she was not only a pretty picture to them, as well? Some people I've told about her seem to not get a thing I say, but others seem to smile and nod when I talk.

But thinking about her, seeing her, touching her, felt like the grandest thing on Earth.

I decided to take it slow, as my heart or body may explode if I thought too hard, if I stared too long. I didn't want to have a love that would turn out to be an obsession in the end.

I have frequently skirted obsession, sometimes falling headlong into it. It is an unrequited love, where you feel like everything was correct, was flawless, but was completely and utterly the opposite.

Lucy and I agreed that that is what Terin felt about Sonya.

Terin did not love Sonya, in fact he seemed to openly acknowledge it. He desired her, but for his own purposes. "Is that how you feel about me?" Lucy asked.

"I don't think so. If I did I'd probably have given up on you long ago. I would've simply seen you, noticed you, and then shut my eyes." I said.

"But what if your other instincts are driving you? What if really it's a necessary human action to be with… a gorgeous woman like myself? Are you sure you're not a vampire, a beast in human clothing, like Terin?" she asked.

I realized she was also questioning my motives, as I was hers. I thought this in actuality was healthy, for we were openly talking about it, instead of hiding it in the dark and growing suspicious and doubtful.

I decided I could make a joke, and evade the question, but I put my hand over Lucy's, and said, "You are very important to me. I think there is a reason for our time together, even if it may simply be for a short while. Even if after all this is over we only have memories." I in actuality couldn't think of a joke, when usually pressed with pressing situations I can think of one on the spot. I wonder if that was a good thing?

She slammed her other hand over mine, and said, "Well. Now that that's settled... Let's read more Terin, shall we? C'mon, we can read together, on the couch."

So we wrapped our arms around each other, and I read over her shoulder, and we picked up where we had left off.

| 35 |

Choosing: Terin

I had this amazing feeling, this sort of mirrored love feeling… I hadn't felt that feeling much, in truth.

I dreamt again, and saw Lucy pictures beside me… drawings of a woman whom I made up.

But that was alright, as she loved me too.

A fiction… a feeling… perhaps a trip in the head? Was I losing my mind, losing it to Lucy?

Would I ever find real love? Was I in love with an idea?

Or is the idea love enough? Would it strengthen me, would it give me more reason to live? Was this a good feeling to have?

I had so many questions… and I asked them to Terin, for he was the only one in my dreams I was talking to, even though he was probably less real than Lucy.

"You see me, in your mind's eye. What am I doing?" Terin said.

"You are just staring… looking at me again, like I know the answer. I told you! I don't know the answer! I'm just asking a goddamned question!" I said.

"What is the answer you seek?" he asked.

"I want this to be good. I want this to be a good feeling... I am dreadfully unsure, and I don't know what is the right path... I just want to be with someone I love..." I said.

"You just want love. Only love. That is alright. We all desire companionship... on this cold road. Why do you think Lucy chose you?" he said.

"I don't know... I thought I chose her..." I said.

"No. She did. Remember that." he said.

"I can't bring myself to tear myself apart. To leave. I want to stay in this dream, forever... this reality. I don't know if I could bear the real world." I said.

"Just take Lucy with you. In your heart... Take her with you... and don't forget..." he said.

And Lucy dragged me out of the dream, and told me to wake up.

| 36 |

The Pool: Terin

Lucy gave me a drawing of herself. Something to remember her by. I was astounded by the work. She said it represented the World in tarot, that that means assured success, change of position, and possibilities. She said she always wanted me to remember that I have options... and that I have her.

She was the World.

And she was travelling the world with me.

I thanked her, and thought of some way to memorialize the picture... ah, I know. A tattoo. I would immortalize it for as long as I had skin to keep the picture on. It would be my gift to her, my gift to myself, and my thanks. I would have to think about it, though. It was a heavy commitment to make. If anything the drawing was nice.

Lucy told me to pucker up... and quit being so depressed.

That was a nice feeling.

So, we walked around Barcelona seeing the old gate. The Arc de Triomf. Originally the arcs were built by the romans, so this one was technically a copy, but it didn't lose value because of it.

We went to a very big park in Barcelona, with big great mermaid statues. There were people dancing and laughing on a stage nearby, amidst the many other people, and we had a mind to join them.

We danced a long time, it was nerve racking doing so, but I was glad we did.

We went back to the hostel, which had a bar. Of course we needed a bar, in a hostel! I think most travellers do after a hard and stressful day of travelling and sightseeing.

I remember before I went to Spain I was alone, and I got in a fight with a U.S. Air Force guy. Only words. Still, I was very drunk and wanted to fight. I had a strong physique, I was drunkenly aggressive and unfrightened. I was picking the fight though... and I regret it. He told me he could kill me. I told him to do it.

I walked away, and he was kind of worried about me, but I just stumbled off to get another drink in the night.

I have a very long history with alcohol.

Although, it's easier when being with someone you trust, that will keep you out of trouble. Like Lucy. Although we sometimes quarrelled when drunk, we didn't really mind the next day, and always would work things out until we were both happy, or happy enough, sometimes long into the night.

I usually drink, smoke, and play games with the other travellers when travelling... but Lucy and I had found something nicer to do together. We read.

It was a good thing we did too, or else we would have nothing to do as the Australian man and (U.S?) woman used our shared hostel room to have sex in. I laughed, as Lucy did, and I closed the door so they could have privacy.

I thought, if I wanted to do it right, I would at least buy a hotel room. The next part of Terin goes thus...

"Terin was in the valley long before Sonya showed a hint of showing herself. But immediately, Terin could sense her, could feel her presence, and soon he could smell her, almost taste her on his lips.

He walked into the moonlight, and this startled Sonya.

Sonya quickly regained her composure and put a good face on, and said, 'My King, you startle me in the evening night... but naught is bad. Your features radiate like ripples in a pond by the moon... and I cannot help but draw close.'

'I have met many like you... but none so beautiful. You bring me close, you draw my desire... I would feed on you, but that... doesn't seem pleasant. Come, follow.' Terin said, speaking bluntly.

Sonya nervously followed him down a path. She knew many men in this area, but she had never seen this spot. This beautiful, radiant pool by moonlight. She gasped as she looked into the water, it was as if it were a mirror in liquid form, so fully still and completely reflecting, down to the minutest flaw.

Terin was undressing, and bid Sonya to do the same.

Sonya sank into the pool, so cool, but not cold, and Terin approached her. 'Bathe.' he commanded.

'Would you wish to feed on me clean? Pure, soft, and unyielding?' Sonya said. She noticed Terin gulp, and she knew the answer in her mind.

'I... I wish to... talk. Yes, talk. We shall talk in this pool.' Terin said, grasping for an answer. He could not think straight as he stared at Sonya. It seemed as if she was the only thing in his senses.

Her scent, like jazmine and roses, her voice, like the sweetest music played by the gods, the sight of her, like the most delicious feast imaginable. He drew close, and touched her skin, like a pillow, but smooth as marble... and the taste of her... Terin could not imagine what the full taste of her must be like...

She stopped his hand as he was feeling her breast.

'Come to the shade with me, King.' she said."

| 37 |

The Blood Flows: Terin

"They talked, it was rather a pleasant conversation, actually. Despite their different positions, as hunter and prey, they were honest with each other, they were open. Terin at first simply desired the unrestrained pleasure that her body and blood could give… but she was drawing on a different pleasure. A pleasure of the mind.

It had been a long time since Terin had that pleasure, if he ever had it honestly in truth.

Old war room games, drunken tavern brawls, speaking formally at dinner with his now dead family. None were remotely similar to this talk between a man and a woman. For that is what they truly were as Sonya revealed to him the many delights of the mind, man and woman. Not vampyr and human, not wolf and sheep, but equals.

They talked, and talked, and talked. Terin sometimes grew frustrated that he could not simply take her life, and Sonya could tell that frustration. He would stare into the pool, into his monstrous features, and sometimes laugh, sometimes snarl, or sometimes shed a single, silent tear. Sonya took him by the arm and turned him to her.

'My King. The night grows short. Let the pleasures in the dark come to a halt, and not be caught unawares by the sun.' Sonya said. Terin hadn't noticed that it was getting early... but frantically, he clothed and left the spot, saying farewell to Sonya. She told him they would meet again."

"You'd think that would be a good time to let him burn up in the morning." I said.

"I think our seductress is being seduced herself. Perhaps she is finding a new challenge? The untamable beast?" Lucy said.

"Maybe. Whelp, let's go to the airport. It's a bit of a hassle, but it'll be easier just flying straight to Germany instead of a bunch of bus rides." I said.

So we left the hostel in the morning, and took the metro to the airport.

We chatted about all the things we saw on the plane. The people we've met, the sights we've seen. They would forever be an adventure locked in our memories. But now, to finish off our trip, we would be going to places where my relatives lived, Germany and Holland. We were getting very tired though, and I thought after we had a few drinks we could take it easy in the Netherlands for a while, then go back home when we were ready. Travelling is one of the most exhausting things you can do.

We ultimately had a few drinks, German beer is one of the best, and walked around Düsseldorf. At first it seemed like there was a lot of trash and beggars about where we got off, but we got to the other side of the city, by the river, and it was rather nice. We saw a bunch of old statues of saints and soldiers, and even went to a few old churches.

Düsseldorf was famed for its mustard, of all things. We had some brats and they were very, very good.

We read, sitting on a bench by the river.

"Terin had gotten into some trouble in his lair. He settled down wherever he pleased, and while he was staying in the house of a, now dead, peasant girl soldiers knocked on his door and demanded to be let in. Terin readied himself as they were about to break down the door.

Immediately, he shot the few with blood bolts, and as the rest were screaming vampyr he chased them down and cut them to bits. But one had escaped. He had sensed nine humans, but only eight were corpses. Terin swore and readied to leave. The city would be in upheaval now, from the accurately superstitious government, from a single soldier's frightened words.

Terin thought that the fun had to start some time.

As he barged into the next peasants' home, and killed them, he had a shuddering shock of paranoia. Could this have been Sonya? Could this have been her doing?

He killed the next household without a second thought, laughing and draining their blood.

But what if it wasn't Sonya?

Terin dropped the corpse to the floor and stopped to think for a second. Would this hurt Sonya? Would this destroy her and her home?

He thought he could go on killing, and as he killed a few more soldiers, sneakily by cutting their throats as they were looking for the sound they just heard, Terin realized he didn't really want this.

He wanted Sonya."

| 38 |

Fractured Light: Terin

I dreamt of showing my family to Lucy, but my family couldn't see her. It was as if she was a ghost in their home. I could not make sense of this. Here was the best girl in the world! But she was a fantasy to all.

Even to me.

I cried on Terin's shoulder, pathetically. I had vowed not to do this, I told myself I wouldn't, but I had dreamed too hard and now…

Reality blurs and fades.

I decided to cut myself short from this feeling, to end this feeling and be done… but Terin said, "Would you wish to die?"

"I… no… I don't wish to die! I just wish to continue my life!" I said.

"Then let Lucy finish hers." Terin said.

"What would you know about it…" I turned and angrily said, "You are words on a page."

"As you are now. I wonder who is reading this… I wonder if it's you, or Lucy?" he said.

"Lucy is a symbol. Just like everything in books are. Just random, meaningless symbols." I said.

"Yet all form into a meaningful person. Into an individual." he said, "Into you. All people are touched by all other things, people are like glass, or diamonds if you prefer, refracting the light of the sun, of the moon, of the inner light of all. Everything is tinted, and comes out as expressions, like words on a page."

"Then I will resume the fantasy, and not linger... although, like all things in my life, in anyone's life, there is always only one sad ending. It is death. Something will have to die, for this to end. Whether it be a feeling, or an individual." I said.

"Read the rest of my book. Tell me what you think the end is." Terin said, and vanished. And I was alone. I realized I had always been alone.

And I woke up.

| 39 |

End?: Terin

Lucy and I went to Holland, and I showed her to my family. They were very impressed with her… but it is hard for me to describe it. It is hard to show someone you love to your family, to have acceptance.

We stayed in a hotel, for once, and finished the book. We were going to go home soon, and we wanted a few days in comfort first. Hostel beds and bus seats can wear you down.

We read, laying on the bed.

"Terin went to meet Sonya. He bid her to leave with him, to flee in the night with him… and if she didn't, he would take her by force.

She knew he was bluffing. She had become incredibly precious to him, a feeling in him that was a delicate flower and required the perfect care, to be gentle with, or it would die. She knew this by the way he grabbed her hand softly and asked, asked instead of commanded, her to leave with him.

Sonya knew also, she had saved many individuals by charming this monster's heart. She had also saved herself, and in a sense, saved Terin.

They stood by the roadside. Sonya asked him if they would die together, if her death is what he still wished.

Terin said that no one has to die… At least she didn't.

Sonya turned to him in the moonlight, her figure was radiant, like a goddess of the evening, for that is what she really was. A goddess in the form of a woman.

And Terin turned to her, he looked like the greatest king, a king of evil, like the Devil. For that is what he really was. A devil, a vampyr, a monster."

And there were no other pages. Someone had torn them out of the back of the book.

I had bought the book at a garage sale, thinking the cover was interesting. I felt cheated.

| 40 |

Finishing a Book: Terin

"I suppose it is just a sappy vampire romance after all." Lucy said.

"Yeah, but... but what about the rest of it!" I said.

Lucy shrugged, and whispered something in my ear.

Her suggestion piqued my interest... It was a way to finish the book.

"I had her underneath my fingertips... in my grasp. I wished to take this flower and keep her forever and ever... but what flower can grow in the dark?" I said.

"I had this beast beneath my palm. Gently holding his face in my hand. I could destroy him, with a simple frown. But I would destroy myself... for I had been tamed, by taming the beast." Lucy said.

"I desired to free myself of this love! To become a beast in the night! But that would not be right. I would forever be chained, chained to this desire, for humanity is the greatest curse one could aspire." I said.

"I wished to lose myself in him. If anything for him to consume me, completely, my last bits of blood sustaining this man... this king. I wished to lose my humanity, to become one with him, and be a beast in the night." Lucy said.

"I wished to see the sun. I wished to see this woman in the radiance of early morn, for her to frolic across the morning dew, and me by her side." I said.

"I wished for some rectification! This should never have been." Lucy said.

"I wished for some rectification! This should have always been!" I said.

"Let sun and moon intertwine, let fantasy and reality converge, let us join, separate, and join again."

I turned off the light, but it was becoming morning.

Some pleasures are better with each other, when light and darkness come together, and we are unsure of who is who, and what is right.

Reality blurs and fades, and reality comes to light, shrouded in the darkness of fiction.

Reality blurs and fades, and the end of a story is never really an end.

| 41 |

Lifting the Veil: Lukas

Lucy had gone home, and I resumed my role as a shadow in her life, a nameless individual. As the writer. I had thought she was the shadow at first.

I do love breaking the mirror, having the mirror reach out and grab you, whilst you look at it. I suppose this story will be a headfirst dive into the mirror.

If you wish to call me by a name, call me Lukas. That is my first name. Get it? Lukas and Lucy? My middle name is Samuel, thus the inspiration for the name Sammy.

Lucy originated from a desire. A desire for companionship, for love, and perhaps finding my talent in writing and not really knowing what to do with it, trying to find a higher purpose. For a desire to create magic, with a few symbols and words.

I suppose every magician must reveal their secrets in the end.

Instead of being a Frankenstein, creating a monster to horrify and create a philosophical discussion on humanity and self, I wished to be an Aladdin and rub a lamp, and make all my wishes come true. I'm not sure if Lucy, as the genie, fulfilled all three wishes as I desired, although there is still one wish left. I suppose I'm saving the last one for the end of this last story.

So let's do a little breakdown on the wishes, first, before we go any further into the mirror.

The first wish, to see a beautiful woman, to bring her alive from my consciousness, to have a dream woman. I didn't even desire to be with this dream woman at the start, I simply wished for her to exist. She does, and doesn't. She forever lives in a book, in my imagination. The wishes genies fulfill can be quite cruel, at times, for I will never truly hold her or talk to her. Perhaps the closest I can get to her is with my dreams, alive or asleep.

The second is the wish to be with this woman, to spend some sort of time with her. I used a lot of my past memories for the trip, but also some of my desires, things I didn't do and wish I did. It was an outline set in my memory, the trip outline, but the memories, or just dreams, spent with Lucy are new. I contrasted her, a realistic fantasy, with a completely fictional fantasy of a vampire. I think I sort of knew I would follow down the romance path for the vampire, and for Lucy, as that is what I desired. I just didn't know it would feel so real, that something set in my imagination could have such an effect on me, and I addressed this in the dream segments with Terin.

Now what could I want with a third wish? The first two were quite fun, and beneficial, but I had a horrible feeling of wanting to die as I ended each story. It was dreadful, but I dreaded that my time with Lucy would come to a close. Perhaps I will simply keep my third wish and not make it, so I will forever have Lucy as the genie, and not let her fade away when my desires are spent. I could simply wish for more wishes, and have our time never end, but I have other dreams that must be fulfilled, and I can't spend my life in a fantasy. Thus this self referential section of lifting the veil. We all must wake up, or close the book, eventually.

But let's dream for a while, thinking about our desires, and find out what we truly desire… what we wish. Let us look into Lucy's Looking Glass, and hopefully not draw the demons of desire to steal our fantasies.

| 42 |

Improving Your Image: Lukas

Lucy has a very negative self image of herself, I suppose that's what first attracted me to her. I wanted to help, to help her find the inner beauty which she has but does not see. Whenever she looks into the mirror, she sees darkness. Does she see me? Am I the negative image?

I suppose I always had a very negative self image. In high school I would work out constantly trying to break this image, to prove to it that I am better than it. But the next day, if I was not sore from exercise, I would have those doubts, that horrible, horrible anxiety, which terrifies me just thinking about. The belief, the knowledge, that you are ugly, and awful, and unfit for love. It truly felt true, if I was not constantly working on this self image.

But now I know, Lucy arose from me, and if I can love Lucy, then I can at least love myself.

So, if I wish something, I wish to at least give Lucy some rectifications to her false belief. Let's start by having her look in the mirror, and we can watch the play that unfolds.

Lucy looked into the mirror.

She saw just Lucy. Her trip had been beneficial, and as she smiled, she remembered all the times she used that smile for happiness. That she truly felt joy with that smile. Her companion always made her smile, by joking, by laughing with her. Lucy thought that her smile was a way to remember him.

He had disappeared from her life… but still, he felt so close. Their last lingering moments excited her mind, excited her body, and she looked at her body and thought, hey, not bad. I got somebody to love it. I guess that means I can love it as well.

She flexed her muscles, on her arms, on her legs. The constant walking around had made her stronger. She realized she never had to be afraid if she kept her body healthy, she would not get sick, she would not be attacked. She could walk, or run, for miles with this strong body. She was happy that her and her companion could improve themselves, together.

Lucy smiled one last time in the mirror, and was happy.

| 43 |

Making Contact: Lukas

I do sort of feel like the villain for my stories, as I am the cause of all my characters' problems. Lucy's friend died, as I wrote down what happened. This made me feel sort of terrible. Did I want her for myself? But with the power of a creator comes certain faults, one is to emulate truth.

I couldn't have a fluffy, blissful fantasy. That would be incredibly boring. I wished for Lucy to be real, to have the faults and doubts that all humans have. So I gave her grief.

Although, I also gave her a way out of that grief, a feeling that it will be alright, in the end.

It is hard being the Devil and God at the same time. Writing, making evil and good at the power of your fingertips, in your own little world that you created just for fun.

But not everything is at a creator's command.

Sometimes it truly felt as if Lucy was putting the words down, making the fantasy, and I was simply following along. I do not understand how the creative mind works, I only have vague notions of the process of it.

I believe I am simply looking at a hidden facet of my life, and writing down what I find. I didn't expect that facet to be populated.

Whole worlds inhabit someone's mind, someone's fantasy. Perhaps we inhabit someone else's fantasy, or are reflections in their mindset. I had said before that I cannot find who Lucy reminds me of, so perhaps she is an alien to me, someone who made first contact and I followed up on. A space traveller, finding new worlds. All space travel finding alien life *has* been a fantasy, so far, so I suppose that could be an apt description.

But now I can talk to this fantasy, this hidden world of Lucy, whenever I like. All I have to do is write a few words and "Lucy said."

"It's still fun being in a book. I think it's the notion of trying too hard is what you feel. That isn't really a problem, just let the voice, my voice, talk as you like, and I can try to explain to all the readers." Lucy said.

Isn't it interesting, making contact?

| 44 |

Gupples: Lukas

So, am I a ventriloquist? Is Lucy my puppet? Perhaps I have the feeling of talking to my puppet, whatever that disorder is called, and believing that she is real. It's the effect of making *you* believe that she is real, is what I'm after.

I am surprisingly lucid in feelings of addressing reality. Drugs, religion, having a disorder called "schizophrenia," have all made me question reality constantly. I've gotten good at shoveling out the bits of real in my life, dividing it from hallucogenic fantasy, and creating my truth. Or breaking that truth as I see fit. Although I know not to go too far, or I may never come back.

But it is all part of the trip, all part of the book, for me to be able to show others a little bit of my fantasy.

"As you can see, he is all other individuals in the book. Hell, he's even me, surprise surprise. But, I have the power to be more. To be a part of someone, something else. To be me. Or even be you. If you decided you wished to talk to someone for an hour, real or fictional, what would you say to me?" Lucy said, "By my words, you perhaps are thinking that I am saying the words as Lucy, but each Lucy's voice sounds different in everyone else's head. Therefore, that Lucy is not *really* me, is she? Or is my tinted voice a part of you? When you read this, you imagine me, but I can look like anyone I desire. I can look like Terin, I can look like Sonya, I can even look like Lukas, making a silly voice. It is difficult finding who is who, when we're all mushed together, in a creator's mind, or in the aspect called life. We all originate from other people, and we all go back to Earth again when we're done."

If someone is colorblind, then they forever see the world in different shades. Their blue isn't blue. Their Lucy isn't mine. Even if everyone can see the pictures of this book, some may still see it differently. Even people who all see things in the same shades have different opinions on the drawings, on Lucy.

Some people can sort of "hear" the words of a book, or see the painted image of a description. Like this, the red and blue bedsheets on Lucy's bed looked nice, and she had just gotten a stunning goldfish and put it on a stand in her bedroom. She called him Gupples.

Others just see words, and simply know what the words say. Even though some see the words and it paints a picture to them, the words can have different meanings as well. Like the word "stunning." Some may see this as flashing lights coming from the goldfish, others simply as an adequately well rounded goldfish, or some may think it looks very gold for a goldfish. There are thousands of words like that in the English language, which are completely up to interpretation how they really describe things. Just like Lucy being up to interpretation.

"So if you're ever stuck trying to create something, remember, it always looks different to someone else. The most important part is the creating bit, and you can find out what you will use it for later. Like a tool, some may see it as useless until the inventor tells you what it is for. Like me, just being a friend to Lukas, or perhaps to you if you need

one. I'm a person just like anyone else, even though I live in a book."
Lucy said.

| 45 |

Experimenting: Lukas

Lucy has sort of been an experiment for me. When I was in the bouts of psychosis, I got too involved in a fantasy, in my writing, and could not tell the truth between reality and fiction. This was when I also started to hear voices. Before you wonder, no, I barely hear voices anymore and I know this is all fiction. It's exactly because it's fiction is why I created it.

My old fictitious story had become reality, the wishes in my head suddenly all became true, because a voice in my head told me so. It was very foolish, but it is unnerving if you start to hear voices. It is very, very unnerving, and very frightening. You lose control. It feels like you never had control. I have control with this, I know I could edit it however I like, and often did.

Reality doesn't give you the same leniency.

I really wanted to see if I could make this fantasy again, with a completely and totally fictional woman, one that has no basis in reality. Thus I put a safeguard on my fantasy, no matter how real it got, it would remain a fiction, as the very basis of it was rooted in fiction. I thought it would be a good exercise in writing, and that is what it started as, although I became enamored with Lucy, and wished to write more, so sort of ran away with the feeling.

"Well, it's not like I had anything else to do, you know." Lucy said.

Yes, but it was completely selfish of me to create without responsibility. Without really knowing what I was going to do with it.

"We all start like that! I was started as a story, as a Facebook post actually, and some girl in California was started because of a drunken night in an abandoned movie theater." Lucy said.

Are you that girl?

"Is that what you wish?" Lucy said.

Haha, no, I'm saving that wish for later.

It doesn't really matter where Lucy came from, how she was conceived. She makes more importance to her story by doing just that, by adding to the story. In this whole realistic fiction called life. That's all anyone can do, as we don't choose our creators, our parents. We *can* choose our god, however. Like Lucy tried to.

| 46 |

In and Out the Void: Lukas

"I feel as if I've been put in the spotlight. I think your own interests in the occult gave me mine. Although it is fascinating, I would never have the belief, the fervor to totally commit. That's like cults and shit. I simply was looking for an easy way out of religion, and not so damning as atheism. I still think there are beliefs that are totally worth learning about, and that we can only learn more about our own, individual, unique beliefs by learning about those of others." Lucy said.

I sort of believe something close to when Lucy was tripping on drugs. That we are all connected, and go back into each other again. We are only everything, everywhere, always, looking in on itself.

"I'm more of an atheist, as Catholicism has failed me time and time again. But, I like Buddhism. I find comfort in believing that the dead are not truly gone." Lucy said.

I actually still find comfort in Catholic prayers. It's my family. They all help keep that belief alive for me, even though I have distanced myself from it, like you.

"We're so similar! You wanted to be with someone who's just like you, but a girl!" Lucy said, smiling.

Well, not *totally* like me. Just someone I could relate to.

"I'm just kidding. Someone who's like me would *be* me. You've given me too many differences, too many beliefs that are not your own. Perhaps you need to make amends to your own beliefs, and accept mine?" Lucy said.

A confusing thought. This is where it's difficult to tell who is who. Who is *really* me. I suppose I would look at it like Terin, being a bloodthirsty murderer. I am not so, nor ever wish to be so. But still, he came from my imagination, some aspect or wish inside of me instilled as a bloodthirsty, violent vampire.

"Which is why we role played as Sonya and Terin. It was a way to show that fiction sort of rubs off on you, and stays alive in you. It was fun, since we could both be different characters, playing different roles from our life." Lucy said.

But alas, this is all me.

It is incredibly lonely, knowing that you're alone. I feel as if I am in a void, but all I have to do is think of Lucy, and I feel better.

"Yuup! That's me, your space ghost traveller lover girl! See, it's not so lonely when you imagine some friends. I think all writers have a sort of loneliness in them, that way." Lucy said.

Religion can be seen as a fantasy as well, and it is much nicer when you know you're not going to die alone, and that you aren't really alone.

| 47 |

Terin and Sonya Talk: Lukas

How about we bring in a different character? One of the ones with names. Hello, Terin, nice to have you here.

"Hello, Lukas. How was the fantasy? Did it play out like you wanted?" Terin said.

Well, I did plan yours. I had a notion of how the ending would turn out, of fiction and reality merging, but your words helped me find it.

"Yes… You are incredibly inept at figuring out the truth. Sometimes you need your subconscious to give you a hand." Terin said.

So you're my subconscious? A vampire, a beast who really only wants a seductress?

"A beast, and like how you put it to distinguish difference, a 'vampyr.' Just a different spelling for vampire. I suppose 'Terin' is just a different spelling for 'Lukas.'"

Quite true. Immediately the dynamic is shifted as I talk to Terin, or to the audience. Lucy is easier to talk to, Terin has taken on the character of being mysterious, an enigma.

"You'll have to do a follow up for me eventually." Terin said.

I think that would be grand. What did you have in mind?

"Oh... I don't know... perhaps an escape from the book. A mystery? The bloodthirsty murderer turns out to be a schizophrenic author?" Terin said, and grinned. He does love to play with my emotions. Yet still, he has been helpful to me. "I think it would do you well to mention Sonya. The hero of the story." Terin said.

Well, sure. Hello, Sonya.

"You do know you barely gave me any dialogue? That's why it's so difficult for you to put me in this talk show setting." Sonya said.

Sorry about that. So what is planned for you two, next? If you could give me a hint... or an idea to be.

"We decided to keep you in the dark for awhile. Let you finish your other dreams before you get back to us. You haven't told us anything about the rest of the stories you're planning." Terin said.

Ah yes. I wish to keep that a secret for now. It will be a grand adventure, a good five or so books, I think. I have four already.

"You mean three and three fourths. Go on! Write something amazing!" Sonya said.

Ok, you've forced my hand.

Sonya and Terin were approaching the sunrise. Terin would accept his fate... would accept the light, but he stumbled, tripped, and as a sun's ray was about to smite him, he was protected by the shade of a tree. The two were like this, eternally locked in the delicate battle of life and death, and Sonya had never been so frightened. He would've willingly sacrificed himself, and now she knew from the feelings that arose in her, he didn't have to.

A little taste of Sonya and Terin.

But this makes my head swim... I prefer a one on one with Lucy, to bringing in every character I've ever created. This is Lucy's Looking Glass, let's keep it focused on her.

| 48 |

The Final Wish: Lukas

"So, how are you going to do this? It makes no sense prolonging the inevitable." Lucy said.

"Yes. Let's just take a break and walk down the path. I like being in the book for a change. I have often times taken on a character's voice as first person, to be them in a sense, and I think I will do this as me." I said.

"Yeah, you're quite silly that way. Maybe you need to make another picture?" Lucy said.

"I *would* like an ending picture. I think I will... although I have no idea of what it could be." I said.

"That self portrait! Make a self portrait!" Lucy said.

"Alright, Luce. Sounds good. I think I should make my wish, although this will undoubtedly be a very short book." I said.

"Not every book has to be Charles Dickens length." Lucy said.

"Yeah... Let's see the page count... looks long enough, I guess."

"Make your wish, then. I'm waiting. I can wait longer, but I believe that you can't." Lucy said.

"I feel so much pressure. I've already wished to create you, wished to be with you, ... I wish to share you." I said.

Lucy smiled, and granted my wish.

So let this be a gift, to anyone who is doubtful, unsure, needs a higher purpose, or is addressing their reality. Lucy is there, and you can talk to her whenever you like.

I looked into the looking glass and saw myself. I knew Lucy would be there, whenever I like. In my heart, where I needed her most.

The End